The Road from Kabul

Angie Faieq

Thank you for reading
and being a part of
the journey!

♡ Angie F

Cover art by Caroline Hein

Printed by CreateSpace in the United States of America

First printing, 2018

ISBN-10: 1986007200
ISBN-13: 978-1986007207

To my father,
for his endless stories,
his courage, and his love

AUTHOR'S NOTE

I have been listening to my dad's stories for my entire life. In many ways, his own experiences have guided me and given me perspective in each decision I make. I have only recently seen his childhood photos and seeing all of those moments and memories was a huge inspiration for me. I spent countless nights sitting with my dad and asking for details, memories, experiences, so I could finally write out his story. Through this book, I have found a home in a country I have never visited and never seen.

As I listened to my dad's stories of coming to the United States, I never realized how much he had to sacrifice for his family. I shared his heartache, felt his fear, understood his pain. I am now a completely different person than I was when I began to write these stories.

Writing this book was difficult, yes, but ultimately one of the most rewarding experiences of my life. I know I will never truly be able to know exactly what my dad has gone through but I have become more connected to him and his culture through my writing. I've been able to challenge myself and put myself in his shoes in a way I never was able to before.

My dad has always told me that one day I would need to write a book about his life because he was never able to do so. Maybe it's difficult to put his own experiences on paper or perhaps he's unable to articulate what he has gone through in English words. Whatever it is, I am honored to be able to relay his experiences in the truest way possible and share the beautiful culture that I have grown up with.

The following essays have been reconstructed from the experiences told by Ahad Faieq. Names have been changed to respect privacy. Details and dialogue have been reconstructed to best match the memories of Ahad.

I
December 24, 1979
Kabul, Afghanistan

Ahad stepped off the bus into Kota-e-sangi Circle, shops buzzing with people. He walked down the street, the smell of lamb dripping out of windows, and watched the hazy sun fading in the cool sky. Kampani Road was full of people, hopping onto the dark blue buses rolling up, markets busy with customers. Jelabi, dried mulberries, and other sweets lined the stands. As the sky darkened, a cold settled over the road and Ahad made his way back to his house, a modest, one-story structure with small windows and earthy-toned brick. Each house was surrounded by tall, thick walls to provide security and privacy to each resident. Walking up to the wall around his own home, Ahad rapped his knuckles against the door and after a moment, his sister Safiya opened the door, her dark eyes downward towards the ground.

"*Salaam*," she mumbled, and Ahad returned the greeting as he stepped through the door into the yard. He passed the garden full of drooping roses and herbs, continuing around to the back of the house, the earthy smell rising to his nose. As he walked around the corner, he saw his room, a small cabin-like structure separated from the rest of the house. He approached his lodge, excited to lie in his bed and let his body rest. However, Ahad paused when he saw his open door. He could hear the low chatter of his family and he glanced back at his sister, who had trailed behind him. Her glazed eyes met his and her rounded face was drained of color. Turning back to the door, Ahad muttered a small prayer for safety before walking in.

Stepping into the room felt like being suspended in water. Ahad's chest tightened when he saw that Omar's face--his best friend, a man who always wore a glowing smile--was solemn. He next saw his mother, watching him with a furrowed brow, her lips pressing together like they had when Ahad first fell off his bike and he came home to her with his knees bloodied. He didn't need to see the rest of his family's faces to know that this was the night he had been planning for months. The night when his entire life would change.

After moving to the main house, everyone sat on the colorful cushions on the floor of the living room, dishing rice and lamb onto their plates. Usual talk was replaced with a haunting silence and Ahad felt the buzz of fear in the air like a swarm of bugs. It was difficult to swallow his food, but he forced down spoonfuls of hot white rice, not knowing when his next meal would be. Omar sat next to him, declining a second helping of lamb from Mariam, Ahad's mother.

"*Lotfan*," she whispered. The word for please in Farsi. Her voice trembled. Omar scooped more rice and lamb onto his plate without another word.

The dinner was followed by heaps of fruit. Ahad grabbed an orange and skinned it, juice dripping down his fingers. He ate the sweet citrusy wedges then glanced at Omar, who had a small helping of dried cantaloupe. Their eyes met. Ahad's heart started to pound as an unspoken understanding passed between them. Omar raised his hand and rested it on Ahad's shoulder. They both stood and the family watched as Omar spoke.

"*Tashakor.*" The word for thank you. "But we must leave now."

Ahad heard some of his siblings whisper prayers; others broke into tears. His mother's face seemed much hollower, her eyes tired and drooping, cheeks wet with tears. Omar handed Ahad a pair of Pakistani clothes. Once Ahad stepped away, he slipped on the long dark brown button up that fell below his knees and loose pants of the same color. The fabric was soft and warm, but he felt like a stranger as he pulled on the vest, and looked down at the garments he would be living in for who knew how long. Ahad pulled out money he had been saving, 750 American dollars wound tightly in a small roll of bills, and tucked it into his briefs. In between the two layers of fabric, there was a small pocket where Ahad slipped the money in. No one but Omar knew he was taking extra money on this trip. He couldn't tell anyone in fear of getting it stolen. He walked back into the main room and saw Omar shaking hands with Ahad's father, Qadir. All eyes turned to Ahad as he approached his family, his long dark hair and his mustache the only familiar things about him. Many of his siblings' eyes widened when they saw him in his new attire.

Ahad took a deep breath and made his way around the family to say his goodbyes. *"Khodahafez,"* Ahad said as he embraced each sister and brother, his mother and father, feeling as if his knees would buckle. The lights in the room now gave Ahad a headache and the smell of food was cold and stale. Earlier, he had walked into his room expecting a relaxing night, but now he was left with a sinking feeling in his chest. With no one else left to say goodbye to, Ahad turned to Omar and they walked out of the house.

As Ahad headed down the street, his family watching him, he saw flashes of his childhood unfolding in front of him. The street he now walked on was the street he used to ride his bike down. He gazed across the road, where he used to play soccer with his school friends on the hot days after school.

Before Afghanistan became a republic, people were happy. Families would travel across the border to sell merchandise. The politics stayed distant from the people's personal lives. In a handful of years, Ahad watched his hometown fall apart. He knew it would never return to the lively town of his childhood. Omar looked over and saw the distant look in Ahad's eyes.

"Ahad Jan," he spoke quietly. This was an endearing term in their language, and between the two of them, it meant family. Ahad looked at his face, Omar's deep brown skin hollowed out by the night. His deep-set eyes peered at Ahad as if he knew his exact thoughts. "There is nothing else you can do."

"*Ma-mehfahmum*, Omar Jan." I understand.

II
December 24, 1979
Kabul, Afghanistan

They arrived at the man's house before midnight. For the entire trip they were silent. But even as they walked through the quiet night, Ahad and Omar were comforted by each other's presence. They walked to Kota-e-sangi Circle and traveled to the house in which Ahad was staying. After months of planning, waiting, and expecting, it was the night for Ahad to leave.

Both Omar and Ahad knew they would likely never see each other again. As Omar knocked, Ahad's head spun. Ravi, the house owner, opened the door, his skin loose around his face, his eyes heavy with dark circles but still full of warmth in the chilled winter night.

"One of you must be Ahad," Ravi said.

"Yes, sir. That would be me."

Ravi gestured them in and led them into a small room with three beds. There, two of Ahad's soccer mates, Khalid and Masood, waited. Since they were in the same position as Ahad, Omar organized the three of them to cross the border together. Ahad wasn't highly involved in the planning because his father, Qadir, disapproved of the idea to leave. Ahad shook the thoughts of his father out of his head. There was no going back.

"Khalid. Masood." Ahad greeted them with an embrace. Khalid and Masood greeted Omar in the same way. The four of them were all closely acquainted and Ahad was glad to have some familiar faces with him through the oncoming journey.

"*Salaam.*" Masood's dark eyes softened with a smile. "I never thought this time would come."

"None of us did," Khalid said.

"It's best to go to sleep now. I don't know when you will leave," Ravi said. Apparently, Ravi knew men who crossed the Pakistan border frequently for business, and had contacted them to help the three friends leave Afghanistan.

"I guess this is it." Ahad turned to Omar, who stood in the doorway of the room. Although Ahad was skilled at controlling whatever he felt, Omar had always seen right through him.

"This day has been a long time coming, Ahad."

"It feels like it was yesterday when we were kids."

"Well, we aren't kids anymore." Omar flashed a grim smile. "I have to go now."

"*Khodahafez*, brother." Ahad smiled and hugged Omar, slapping his hand on his back.

"*Khodahafez*," Omar replied and waved at Khalid and Masood as he stepped away. Ahad wished Omar could leave Kabul. However, since Omar was married, he wouldn't be able to take his wife along. There was a slim chance a woman could cross the border without suspicion. Omar was also on better terms with the government and there was no pressing need for him to leave.

Ahad looked over to his two other friends. "When are the other men coming?"

"No idea," Masood replied.

"Then we should get some sleep," Ahad said. They both nodded in agreement as they lay down in their beds. Ahad laid his head on the pillow. He tried to push away the thoughts of home. As Ahad shut his eyes, he tried to convince himself he was in his own bed. However, everything around him felt alien.

After about an hour, Khalid and Masood were asleep. Ahad lay on his back, eyes staring at the blank ceiling. He recalled the expressions on his family's faces, solemn, quiet, pale. He said all of their names quietly under his breath, each syllable feeling more and more foreign in his mouth. A pain edged behind his brow and he sat up, squeezing his hooded eyes until he saw spots behind his lids.

He recalled everything that had led him to that moment. When the king was overthrown. When political groups began to rally. When everyone became silent. Ahad was in college when this all began to happen. No one talked about the government. There were people who disappeared after speaking their disapproval of certain officials. Soldiers came into Ahad's school and took classmates away. Friends disappeared. Every day felt like a risk. Then, the curfew was put into place. Nights were filled with the drone of planes. Markets became more infested with Russian soldiers every day. Ahad's head pounded from the memories.

He looked up to the ceiling and started to pray.

"*Bismillah-e-rahman-e-rahim.*" In the name of Allah, the most gracious, the most merciful. His voice was rough and he wished he had remembered to bring his cigarettes. Holding his hands open, he rested his head in his palms and offered everything he had become, everything he had experienced, to God.

III
December 25, 1979
Kabul, Afghanistan

Ahad woke up to Khalid shaking him. Grunting, Ahad pulled himself up and looked at the thin face of his friend. "They're here," Khalid whispered. Ahad, suddenly feeling wide awake, followed Khalid to the front door. The night was still and Ahad guessed it was the early hours of the morning. Ravi waited with two other men and Masood.

Ahad glanced at the two strangers, feeling like an animal inside a cage. One man wearing a turban had his gaze fixated on Ahad. His demeanor was intimidating: tall with a heavy stare and an upright posture that let everyone in the room know that he meant business. The other man, shorter, with neatly cut hair, stood with a more pleasant expression, his face relaxed into a soft smile as he clasped his hands together in front of him.

"This is Hamid and Isah." Ravi gestured to the two men.

"This won't work." Hamid, the man with the turban, spoke first, and raised a finger towards Ahad.

Ahad tried to speak but his mouth felt like he swallowed sand. He coughed and forced out a word. "What?" Could he not leave?

"Your hair," Isah said. Grabbing Ahad by the shoulder, Hamid led him further into the clay house. Behind him, Ahad could hear Isah asking if Ravi had scissors. Ahad stood in the main room as Ravi brought out a large pair of scissors. The blades glinted in the dim lantern light. Ahad took them and glanced around. No mirror. The men around him watched expectantly.

With a deep breath, Ahad took a chunk of hair with his left

hand and raised the scissors above his head. With no way to see what he was doing, Ahad closed his eyes and snipped. He repeated the movement several times blindly on top and around his head, trying to feel the evenness of the cut with his free hand. His dark hair fell to the ground in clumps. When he needed to do the back of his head, he handed the scissors to Masood, who trimmed the back with ease. When Ahad's hair was finally short, he ran his hand across his head and felt the messiness of the new cut. Ahad sighed. Yet another thing he'd leave behind.

Ahad handed the scissors back to Ravi, and looked over to Hamid and Isah. They held three pieces of paper in their hands. Khalid, Masood, and Ahad took the papers and glanced them over.

"These are letters." Hamid's voice was low. "I was able to throw some money around to get them, so do not lose them. Do you understand?" His eyes hardened and he stared at the three friends. "This is your excuse to cross the border. You need to memorize these names on the paper. One will be your identity and the other will be your father's identity. These will get you passage through the checkpoint. If anyone asks, you are crossing the border so you can get meat for the army to ship back to Kabul."

Ahad looked over the letter. Its ink was slightly blotted, and a scrawled signature embellished the end; Ahad was able to make out the letters to the name of a government official. He read the letter and skimmed through it a few times before he could hear the restlessness in the room. He folded it and tucked it into the chest pocket of his new attire.

"And take this." Isah held out money. Glancing up, Ahad opened his mouth in protest, but realized he would be better off accepting what was given. "You'll need to hide this somewhere inconspicuous."

Ahad, Khalid, and Masood each took a small amount of money. It was about 900 Afghanis and Rupees, the currency of Afghanistan and Pakistan respectively, just enough for bus fares and other small costs for the trip across the border. He slid the money and the letter in his shirt pocket, muttering a soft *"tashakor"* as his eyes fell to the ground. Ahad longed to be home. He wished he was a child again, riding his bike through Kabul without a single fear slowing him down. However, Ahad pushed away these thoughts and focused on the issue at hand. Ahad's life was on the line. He couldn't afford to be distracted. After the three got ready to leave, Hamid and Isah led the men out of the house. Masood turned to Ravi and bowed his head slightly in thanks. In return, Ravi gave a smile and sent them off into the cold night.

As Ahad stepped outside, he ran his broad hand through his hair. Its unfamiliar shortness left his ears exposed to winter gusts.

"Do the three of you speak Pashtu?" Hamid asked.

"I'm not fluent but for the most part, yes," Khalid said. Masood nodded in agreement.

"I know a few phrases but I can't speak it very well." Ahad dropped his gaze, knowing this would only make it that much more difficult for him. In Pakistan, if he was stopped at the border, people would start asking him questions in Pashtu, their main language. Just by not knowing the language he would be sent back to Afghanistan.

Hamid and Isah exchanged quick glances then led them to a taxi car, the one in which Hamid and Isah had arrived, waiting on the road. They climbed in, Hamid and Isah in the front next to the taxi driver and the three friends cramped into the back. The car seats were cold, and, as Ahad sat, he folded his hands to warm his fingers.

There was very little talking in the car. Hamid told the driver to travel to Jalalabad and the man started the car and pulled away from Ravi's house. Ahad stared out the window as the car drove away from the town. Outside, Ahad could barely see the cliffs in the darkness. He felt his heart beating steadily in the still night as he thought about his family. This was it. Ahad was really leaving. He shut his eyes to remember their faces, their solemn expressions when he walked into his room. Guilt flooded his chest and he felt a knot in his stomach. He took a deep breath and prayed.

Once they got to Jalalabad, Ahad stopped in a shop to buy a pack of cigarettes. It was early in the morning as they boarded a bus to travel to Torkham, the town near the border. After the five found seats, the bus pulled away from the stop and Hamid turned to the three friends and whispered, "When we get to the border, Isah and I will show you ways to get across. Ahad, you will have to be cautious; you look very unlike Pashtun locals. Cutting your hair is only half of a disguise." Ahad nodded and looked out the window, his entire body feeling empty and weak. Ahad knew he looked different than the Eastern Afghans. He had lighter skin, a flatter face, hooded eyes, and he knew that although Omar had gotten him clothes similar to those worn in Torkham, it wasn't enough to mask his contrast from the locals.

Ahad pulled out the letter from his shirt pocket and looked over the names again, whispering them under his breath. These letters were supposed to be for three other young men, actual soldiers, who had to get meat for the army. Instead, Ahad and his two friends were taking their place. In Afghanistan, everyone was known by their name and their father's name; that was how people traveled and made connections. If one of them messed up the names, all this effort would be for nothing. Ahad muttered the names to himself like a prayer and heard Masood doing the same.

The sky was bright and the sun glowed brightly above the mountains. Ahad tried to sleep but couldn't; instead, he watched the buildings and landscapes smoothly pass out of sight. The enclosing valleys and hills outside looked like sand dunes and he let his mind wander.

He pitched into small conversations every now and then, only vaguely listening to the chatter about the soccer season and family. He tapped his fingers on the back of his other hand, the rhythmic, steady beat somehow easing his nerves. If Ahad made it to the United States, a whole new chapter would open for him. He thought about the cities he would see, the people he would meet, and the possibilities of life there. However, Ahad knew it wasn't as simple as his fantasies. It wasn't a question of when he would get to America, it was a question of if he would make it.

After a few hours, the bus rolled to a stop, finally reaching Torkham. It was the afternoon and the passengers got off while Ahad's mind buzzed from lack of sleep.

Hamid looked at the young friends as the bus rolled away. The air was thin and cold and each breath felt uncomfortably dry. Ahad gazed around. They now stood on the side of the road, by a few desolate buildings, colorful trucks occasionally driving by. The town they were in was near the border of Pakistan. In the distance, Ahad could see the border checkpoint: a gate with a thick metal chain to prevent trucks from passing through. Swarms of soldiers crowded around the checkpoint, searching the vehicles that drove up.

The sun was high in the sky and Ahad felt no hint of his previous exhaustion. Now, his insides were buzzing and there was a constant tension in his lungs. Being so close to the border alarmed Ahad. He was about to become a fugitive and the idea was difficult to grasp. Soon, Ahad would be risking his life. He wondered if he would ever see his family again.

"You both will have to escape separately. These trucks," Hamid gestured as one bumbled down the road, "come along to cross the border often enough so you'll have plenty of chances to get across. I'm going to talk to the drivers and convince them to let you hide on top or inside of the truck. If that doesn't work, well…we can figure that out later." He shifted his eyes to Khalid and Masood. "You both look like locals. You can easily sit in the front seat and pass through. If you get past the border, you'll be able to blend in with the townspeople to hide until we can leave. Ahad, you'll need to stay hidden."

The two names escaped from Ahad's lips one last time as he met Hamid's gaze. Fear swelled in his throat, and he thought he could vomit at any given moment.

"Are you three ready?" Isah asked.

"Yes," Khalid said. His voice was full and firm as if he had prepared for this moment his entire life. If he was nervous, it didn't show. Masood nodded and pressed his lips together.

"Ahad?" Hamid glanced to him.

Even with the brisk winds, Ahad felt hot, sweat sticking to his calloused hands. Hands that had supported his younger siblings. Hands that lifted the furniture as his father's back grew stiff. Once steady hands that now trembled. He looked into Hamid's dark narrow eyes and inhaled deeply.

"Yes."

IV

1970

Kabul, Afghanistan

It was about six in the morning. The sun was just rising and Ahad was wide awake. His entire family was crowded around Qadir's car, packing it full of fresh vegetables, rice, meat, and other food they had bought that morning. Ahad had been looking forward to this weekend for days. Every once in a while, his family would travel to Paghmaan, a garden nestled below the mountains just north of Kabul. It was beautiful there: vibrant flowerbeds, fruit trees, and statues made of marble. A place right out of a story book. Families waiting for hours before it opened just to get a good spot to set up camp with intricately designed carpets, cushions, and pots.

Once everything was packed, they drove for an hour and got to the Paghmaan gardens. They found a place on a grassy piece of land shadowed by the canopy of tall trees towering above them. Close to them, a stream fed by the melting snow from the mountain peaks, the water so crisp and cold that if Ahad kept his hand in for too long it would go numb.

Unpacking, the women set up the carpets and cushions on the ground while Ahad's siblings took the fresh fruit, the melons, cherries, and grapes, and put them in containers, carrying them to the river. Ahad made a little dam with stones that created a pool of the rushing water and placed each container of fruit in that small basin. This kept it fresh until lunch. Ahad wished they could store food like that all the time. Brothers carried stones to the camp for the fire. Back over at the campground, the fire was ready for cooking the meat and rice, smoke rising from the crackling branches.

His mother was one of the best cooks in Kabul. Food full of flavor and texture. Rice always garnished with carrots and raisins and the meat cooked to perfection. The smell of dinners after coming home from school always made Ahad's mouth water. She cooked the lunch with the clean, sharp water from the stream. It made the rice taste sweet and earthy, a flavor the entire family loved. The tastes so fresh and natural, it felt like the purest food on earth.

Ahad passed the time by playing cards and taking walks around the gardens. In these moments, there wasn't a sense of time. Worries vanished into the crisp, clean air. His mind felt as clear as the stream water that rushed shallowly over the eroded stones. These weekends were bliss. He felt the energy from the earth around him, life radiating out of every tree. To him, these were the times where he felt most connected to Allah.

Finally, lunch was ready. Familiar warm smells of spicy lamb and sweet raisins. Ahad and his family sat on the cushions and ate, indulging in each savory bite. Then, the fruit: fresh and cold from sitting in the water. Fingers stained with red cherry juice, adults lost in boring conversation. Ahad ran off with his brothers to play soccer and volleyball.

Later in the day, Ahad's father, Qadir, was giving some money out to the kids to buy some sweets from shops down the road. The children sat around Qadir on the vibrant carpets, a silver coin in his hand. A gunshot. Qadir shouted out in pain. The coin no longer in his hand. The smell of burning wool. The kids looked around in panic. A bullet burning a hole into the carpet. Blood dripping from Qadir's thumb. His palm indented with a red circle from the coin he was holding seconds before. The coin, sitting near Ahad, the metal bent.

Qadir stood and went to the river to wash his hand. Ahad saw his father's thumb split down the middle. Then, Qadir wrapped it with a scrap of cloth and the family left Paghmaan. The children were ushered home.

Hours later, Qadir returned with six stitches down the length of his thumb. He was never able to bend that thumb again. Ahad asked what happened. Reckless hunters, Qadir said. Ahad realized if his father had been sitting a few centimeters to the left, he would have died.

Ahad dreamed of blood. He saw his own hand, blown clean off. Despite the sleepless nights, Ahad always held on to that experience. That moment was a reminder they were all alive and well. He took the gardens, his family, the fruit, for granted. It was a sign, surely, a sign from God telling Ahad to be grateful for what he had, because there would be so much more complexity in his future.

V
December 25, 1979
Torkham, Afghanistan

Ahad leaned on the side of a building, smoking a cigarette. The sun had risen and was bright in the clear sky, but Ahad felt none of its warmth. The smoke of the cigarette seeped into his chest until he exhaled. In the distance, a truck started to roll up the street. Like the others, it was covered in bright illustrations, intricate designs lacing across its tall structure. Brief verses were painted delicately on the side in vibrant hues of pink, yellow, and blue. He glanced over at Hamid who stood across the road and gave Ahad a small nod. Stubbing out the cigarette, Ahad walked slowly to the roadside, and saw Khalid waiting across the street. Masood was already on the other side of the border, since he had gotten across on his second try.

Hamid jogged into the street, and brought the truck to a stop. Ahad approached him as he began a conversation with the driver, a dark man with a grim face and a turban.

"He needs to get across." Hamid explained, pointing at Ahad.

The driver, eyes looking Ahad up and down, gave a reproachful look and paused before answering. "I have better things to do." His voice was deep and rough.

"I can pay," Hamid offered. Pulling out some cash from his pocket, Hamid showed it to the driver who flicked his eyes between the money and Ahad. The hesitation felt immensely heavy in the air as Ahad held his breath.

"Fine. Climb up onto the top." The driver took the money and tucked it away in his clothes as Ahad gave Hamid a look. They walked over to the back of the truck and Ahad grabbed onto a bar of metal that hung above the truck doors. He pulled himself up to the roof and before he hid he looked down at Hamid.

"I'll see you on the other side, then." Ahad raised his eyebrows.

"Let's hope it's that easy," Hamid responded.

Ahad crawled to the front of the cargo bed towards the driver. The sides of the bed and a short awning on the end could hide Ahad from soldiers. His heart raged inside of his chest as the truck began to drive. The rumbling of the wheels against the road drowned out Ahad's uneven breath. His spine hurt from laying down in the small corner. The truck rolled on for a few minutes before he felt it settle to a stop. The border crossing.

He could see what was happening in his head as the soldiers started speaking in Pashtu. He could understand only a few phrases, so he shut his eyes to concentrate.

"What are you..."

"...carrying anything?"

"...a few weeks?"

"...your name..."

Footsteps fell around the truck. The doors to the back of the truck opened. Men rummaged around the cargo the driver was carrying. Ahad forced his breath to be shallow. His short fingernails dug into his palms, pinpoints of pain stinging his hand. What if the driver betrayed him? What if he just took the money and told the soldiers there was a twenty-something man hiding on top of his truck? Another minute passed. The back of the truck slammed shut, and Ahad heard the small clang of the metal chain being let down. Then, the truck continued. Now Ahad was in Pakistan. He would only need to pass through a gate before he could get off.

A wave of relief flooded Ahad's body. His muscles relaxed

and he took a deep breath. He was past the border. Thoughts ran through his mind like oil being fed to an engine. He couldn't believe it was this easy. There was no way he could have gotten past the border already. The cool sense of relief seeped over his chest but there was another feeling. Something heavy in his throat that Ahad couldn't swallow. He realized that there was now a definitive line dividing him from Afghanistan. Ahad didn't think he would ever step foot in his hometown again.

Pushing the thoughts aside, Ahad listened carefully to hear the truck pass the second batch of soldiers waiting by the road leading into Pakistan. He thought he heard a voice fade so he peeked over the truck bed and saw the gate growing smaller as the truck drove on. He got up and climbed over the side of the truck, holding onto the roof, then let himself hop onto the ground. The shock of impact shot up his ankles as he landed and fell to his knees. He had gotten off the truck as planned. Now, he needed to find some place to wait until Hamid, Isah, and Khalid were across the border.

Ahad stood and brushed off his pants before walking along the road. Townspeople glanced at him; a man with deep-set eyes, sitting on the ground against a building, watched him with a hardened gaze. He focused on the road and after spotting Masood near a closed shop, he walked towards the familiar face. There he would be able to shake the feeling of stares from the townspeople. But before Ahad could even catch Masood's attention, a hand grabbed his shoulder.

Ahad turned, his stomach tightening. The man who was just sitting now stood before him, hand gripping his shoulder. The man's face was menacing. It was as if he was about to tear Ahad apart limb by limb. Fear caught in Ahad's chest and he didn't dare to breathe. This man could have been a soldier. He could have had a gun tucked somewhere in his clothes. At any second

Ahad thought the man would kill him and he could only think of his family, their faces once they heard the news Ahad was dead.

He began to speak in Pashtu. "What are you doing here?"

Ahad, barely able to understand, couldn't form the sentence in Pashtu. The man's gaze hardened.

"You need to leave."

Hand still on Ahad's shoulder, the man led him back to the checkpoint without a word, where Ahad crossed the border back into Afghanistan and walked behind a building to Hamid. Disappointment weighed down Ahad's every step.

"Made it through but I got caught in the town," Ahad commented in a flat voice, leaning against the wall.

"It's never the first try."

Ahad sighed. He was already fatigued and only wanted to lay down in a warm bed. Every instinct in his mind was telling him to give up. However, he thought of his family and what would happen to them if he did travel back to Kabul. Ahad would never be able to show his face in his hometown again. He was a fugitive now. A fact with which he would have to live.

VI

December 25, 1979
Torkham, Afghanistan

As Ahad waited, Khalid and Isah spoke to one of the Pakistani truck drivers. Khalid hopped into the front seat of the truck and Isah walked back to behind the buildings. Feeling stiff and cold, Ahad pressed his lips together as he watched the truck drive towards the border. The desolate buildings around Ahad looked pale, a mirage blending in with the gray sky. It was nearing evening.

While Ahad waited for another truck, he adjusted his clothes, the hem of his shirt, the wrinkles of his pants. He heard a low grumble and a truck rolled into view. Ahad looked over to Hamid who started to approach the truck. Then Hamid gave the driver money and Ahad climbed on top of the vibrant truck, hiding in the bed as he had before. He breathed gently as the truck started to drive. If he did it once he could do it again.

When the truck came to a stop, he heard a similar conversation exchanged, the steps, the rummaging. However, he felt the truck shake as men pulled themselves to the roof. A new noise of boots against metal clanged against his ears. He could feel the metal vibrating as soldiers stood on the top. His heartbeat quickened and he held his breath, trying to shrink into the corner. He shut his eyes and prayed. The voices of these men were new, louder, more resentful. Ahad felt the air tremble with each bark of a command. His lungs screamed for air but he refused to take a breath.

Suddenly, he felt a hand clamp around his wrist, the fingers gripped tightly around him as he sharply inhaled. He bit down on his tongue as he was yanked out from his hiding spot, and the metallic taste of blood flooded his mouth.

Ahad's mind spun as he imagined what could happen next. If he was caught, he could be killed. Worst case scenario. It was definitely possible. The soldiers had guns and they dealt with this kind of business frequently, even more often now that the government was in shambles. Ahad could be sent back to Afghanistan, where he would immediately be arrested, charged for espionage. His family would be questioned, possibly even punished for harboring a fugitive. Ahad swallowed the blood pooling in his mouth. Maybe being shot wasn't the worst case scenario.

The man who had grabbed him had strong dark features, with a thick beard. He pulled Ahad off the truck and led him towards the building near the border checkpoint. Ahad felt something hard jab into his back and from a small click, he knew it was a gun. As he tried to turn and see if his suspicions were right, the man shoved him and brought a Russian machine gun under his chin. Ahad's jaw clenched, the cold stinging his eyes as his head throbbed with panic. He was brought to another soldier outside of the building who started to pat him down. Ahad's breath caught when the man's hand lingered over the fold of Ahad's briefs. Ahad hoped he wouldn't search everywhere because if he saw Ahad's savings, that would be a red flag. He glanced down to see the man's narrow eyes.

"What is this?" The man said, pressing his finger against the fold of the fabric resting on Ahad's hip.

Ahad tried to gather his thoughts, to spit something out, but the only thing he was aware of was the gun pressed to his neck. "*Chota*," Ahad choked out. The word for briefs in Farsi. He tried to keep his voice steady as the cold barrel pressed against his exposed skin. The man gave Ahad a suspicious glance before continuing to search. He pulled out the letter and money Ahad was given and tucked the 900 Afghanis and Rupees in his own clothes. He held the letter and said, "I'll show our supervisor." The man ran inside of the building and after a few tense minutes, returned with another man in a different uniform with a gun belted to his side. The supervisor held Ahad's letter and began to read it over. Ahad held his breath, not daring to make the slightest movement. The air was still. The only sound was the wind and the faint hum of the trucks driving through the border. Ahad wondered if Hamid and Isah were still waiting for Ahad.

Finally, the supervisor looked up at Ahad with narrowed eyes. "What are you doing here?"

Ahad swallowed. "I'm here to buy meat for the army in Kabul."

"What's your name?"

He almost didn't hear the question as the blood pounded in his ears. "Ali Saqqaf," he said. Ahad was glad he had repeated the names from that letter as much as he did.

"And your father?"

"Amjad Saqqaf, sir."

"You know who signed this, yes?"

"Yes, sir."

"So you should know we can't let you through like this."

Ahad said nothing.

"We don't deal with your business this easily."

"I was sent over to help the army, sir." The gun pressed harder against Ahad's neck, making him bite down on his lip.

"Then go back to Jalalabad and get another letter. Then we can take you across to Pakistan and help you do what you need to do." A grave expression plastered across the man's face. Ahad couldn't move and when he tried, the gun bit into his skin. His breath became jagged and rough. The man stared at him and said something to the soldier who held the gun. The barrel dropped but his grip on Ahad's arm tightened.

Ahad couldn't get another letter because it wasn't addressed to him. If the soldiers didn't accept this letter, there was no way Ahad could make it across the border.

After several moments in silence, the supervisor held out the letter. "Get another letter, then we can help you."

Ahad grabbed the paper without looking down at it. "Yes, sir." His voice stayed flat, monotone, as he tried controlling the shaking in his words. He wanted to scream, to make a run for it and hope for the best. "Could I have my money back?" Ahad said through his teeth. The man nodded to the soldier who searched Ahad. With a glare, the soldier returned the money to Ahad. Then the supervisor nodded to the soldier with the gun who hovered over Ahad like a vulture over prey. The soldier led him back towards the road, the barrel of the gun poking into Ahad's back until they reached the bus stop far from the border line. Ahad barely noticed that the day had diminished into evening.

"Don't think about pulling this stunt again," the soldier threatened.

Ahad watched the soldier walk away into the dark then snuck behind a building. He leaned against the clay wall, letting out a deep sigh.

Ahad couldn't see Hamid or Isah anywhere. He assumed they had crossed the border to avoid being associated with Ahad while he was questioned and searched. He sank down into a sitting position and rubbed his hand across his face. Now, he was alone and had to find a way to cross the border. Though, he was still rattled from the previous events, so he let his mind wander, retreating into memories that were much warmer, much safer, than the town he was in now.

He let his mind drift back to the simpler days. Days when he and his father would go hunting in the mountains. Days when his only worry was whether or not he was staying out too late. Ahad retreated into his memory and stayed there until his heart-rate returned to normal.

In the night, Ahad pulled out the pack of cigarettes. He wondered if he would ever see Hamid and Isah again and looked around at the vacant alley, feeling separated from the safety of his friends.

VII

December 25, 1979
Torkham, Afghanistan

Ahad spent the time watching people walk through the town, passing clay houses and small shops, bags weighing their arms down. Soldiers hovered between him and the checkpoint to ensure he wouldn't trespass again. They knew his face now. The winter night settled onto the sky and the fading light left Ahad with an uneasy feeling. He squinted to see a small boy playing with his brother as they both trailed behind their parents. The brothers pushed each other and they laughed, the giggles echoing in the air.

In the still night air, he wondered if his father was right. Maybe Ahad didn't need to leave. There were hundreds of people staying behind in Afghanistan. However, Ahad recalled the Russian soldiers. Back home, Ahad was too involved with the Westerners at the American Cultural Center. The soldiers saw him as a threat. They had followed him, searched the cars and houses of his American friends. Ahad couldn't be seen in public without catching the eye of a Russian soldier. There was no other choice but to leave.

His thoughts were broken up by the familiar rumbling coming up the hill. He knew this was his chance. The uneasiness in his stomach spiked. If he didn't get on this truck now, he didn't know when his next opportunity would come.

The truck pulled up to the checkpoint and soldiers began to search through its cargo. Ahad walked up near the chained gateway and he saw it all play out in his mind. He would have to wait until the truck was cleared before running onto it since hiding on top of the truck didn't work. Ahad hoped the driver wouldn't stop and let the soldiers grab Ahad. There was no way of telling what would happen but there was no other choice. Now that the soldiers were aware refugees were crossing on top of the trucks, all trucks were being thoroughly searched before passing through.

Ahad stayed hidden behind the corner of a building and watched the truck from the corner of his eye. The soldier who had led him back to the buses was talking to the driver. As Ahad heard the clang of the chain, he readied himself. The truck was a good eighty meters away and his mind was buzzing with adrenaline. The truck began to drive away so Ahad took off.

As Ahad sprinted forward, his calves began to cramp and it felt like his vision blurred, but he knew exactly where he was going. The soldiers' voices began to clash in the air. Ahad dodged a man lunging at him, hopped, and jumped onto the back of the truck, holding on to the bar of metal that hung above the doors. As soon as Ahad grabbed onto the back of the truck, the vehicle sped off. He had a moment of relief when he realized the truck driver wasn't going to stop for the soldiers. He pulled his body flat against the truck doors and the soldiers' shouts started to clear up in the mass of voices.

"We're going to shoot you!" This was a phrase Ahad could clearly make out from the Pashtu chatter. He heard the click of guns, but the shouts grew quieter. He put his head down as much as he could, not daring to look in case he would be staring down rifles. However, as the truck continued to drive, he opened them anyway and what he saw confirmed his fears. In the diminishing light he could see the glint of metal. He flinched at the soldiers' shouts, thinking their voices were gunshots. Ahad wondered if he should let go. Maybe his life wasn't worth it. Maybe this was a sign. But even if Ahad wanted to let go, his hands felt as if they melted into the metal. As he watched, the soldiers' faces faded in the distance. They didn't run after him. There was no gunshot.

His heart felt like it wasn't beating at all. Feeling started to seep back into Ahad's body and he noticed a pinching in his knuckles. He lifted his head and looked at his hands that gripped the metal bar. The veins popped out from the back of his hand so he relaxed his fingers and let the blood rush back into his fingertips.

The night hung over the sky as the truck rolled closer to the gate into the Pakistani town. Ahad could hear the soldiers' voices and he froze. He had forgotten about the second checkpoint. Now that the truck was within the soldiers' sight, Ahad couldn't climb onto the top. So he remained still as the truck sped through the gate. He pressed his body against the metal as he passed the group of soldiers.

Maybe it was the night, the color of his clothes, or even Allah's blessing, but the soldiers couldn't see him. Since the truck didn't stop, the soldiers didn't have a chance to see Ahad. He exhaled, not realizing he was even holding his breath. When the truck was out of sight from the gate, the driver slowed and Ahad hopped off of the truck. Ahad wanted to thank the driver for helping him cross the border but the truck was already driving away.

Around Ahad, townspeople watched him, so he walked along the side of the road and kept a steady pace to avoid causing suspicion. He passed many people who gave him wary looks, but after a few minutes of walking, he finally saw Hamid, Isah, and his two friends.

When he approached the group, Masood's face lit up. Ahad could see his smile even in the dark. He walked up to him and they embraced, all of them grateful to be alive and together. "Glad to see you, in one piece," Khalid said.

"Same to you," Ahad replied.

"We should get going. It's a long ride to Peshawar," Hamid interrupted.

VIII
December 25, 1979
Peshawar, Pakistan

The five men continued down the road crowded with shops, until they came to a bus stop. They boarded a bus and each of them paid for their own fare. Ahad, Khalid, and Masood used the money Hamid and Isah had given them before. There were many other people on the bus, which put Ahad on edge. They all grabbed a seat, and leaned their heads against their chairs, letting out deep breaths. Ahad listened to the gentle humming of the bus engine and noticed how heavy his body felt against the seat. He let his mind drift away and fell into a limbo of sleep, dreaming faintly of summer days in Kabul.

"Ahad Jan." Masood's voice woke Ahad. "Look."

"Oh, let him sleep, Masood," Khalid said.

Ahad's eyes wavered open with a bit of annoyance. However, when he opened his eyes, a city glowed before him. Ahad could see the lights of shops and homes spill into the night. The sight faded into the distance and vast stretches of farmland took over the landscape. The five men stared out the window for the rest of the ride, cautious not to draw attention to themselves. Ahad's eyes kept flicking over to the other passengers, and he wondered what could have possibly brought them this far at such a late hour. When a woman looked up and met Ahad's eyes, he felt a panic in his chest as he realized they could be thinking the same thing about him. He started to tap his fingers again and mulled over prayers in his mind.

He prayed for his family's safety. He wondered when he would see the faces of his siblings next, or whether he would ever see Omar again. If Ahad knew his goodbye to Omar was the last time seeing his best friend, Ahad would have said much more. Though, when Ahad tried to think of what he would have said, he realized his friendship with Omar surpassed all words.

The bus pulled into Peshawar, and the passengers got off. Ahad and the other men walked down the road, past the shops until they left the small city. On the side of the road, a couple *rekshas* waited, small vehicles Ahad saw often, with open doors and benches to casually transport people around town. The *reksha* could only hold two to three people so they had to take a few to travel.

"*Salaam*," The driver said when the group approached.

Hamid and Isah rode one *reksha* while Masood, Ahad, and Khalid squeezed into another.

After about an hour of driving, the *rekshas* pulled into a neighborhood. They each paid the drivers and started to walk towards a house.

"Where are we?" Masood asked.

"A house where you can stay safely until you're able to leave Pakistan," Isah responded.

"Will you both be staying, as well?"

"Sadly, no. We have other business to take care of," Hamid said.

The neighborhood was packed with lines of houses along a narrow road. They approached a house with double doors and walked up to the entrance. Khalid was the one to knock. His hand rapped gently against the door, followed almost immediately by a couple opening the doors.

"*Salaam*," Hamid greeted with a smile and embraced the couple as if they were family. The man was middle-aged with a thick, dark beard, the light from the house reflected off of a few strands of silvery hair. The woman was pinch-faced, thin lips and large dark eyes, her smooth chestnut skin giving off a glow that made her appear younger than she was.

"This is Ahad, Khalid, and Masood." Isah gestured to the three young men.

"Nice to meet you. I'm Bahram."

As Ahad stared at the couple, he could barely comprehend the risk Bahram was taking to house three refugees. They must have children, a family. If Ahad, Khalid, and Masood were discovered, Bahram and his wife would lose their home, their land, their money, and maybe even their lives.

"Alright, boys. This is where we get off," Hamid said.

"*Tashakor*, Hamid. For everything." They all shook hands.

"You three are bright young men. I'm sure your lives are full of promise." Isah nodded at them before turning and walking back to the taxi.

"Good luck to you. You won't be able to leave the house for a while because you can't be seen. Do you understand?" They nodded and Hamid slapped their shoulders and smiled. "*Khodahafez*," he said and waved at Bahram and his wife.

"Please don't stand in this cold, come in." Hamid spoke in Pashtu and pulled the three inside, leading them through another door on the right that led into a large room with five beds. Ahad glanced at the empty cots and wondered who had stayed here before. The walls were faded and blank, the floor dusty and uneven. The beds were spaced evenly across the furthest wall, all draped with beige sheets stained with age. There were no windows and a small end table stood near the door. The three claimed their beds and Ahad wished he were back home.

"We've made it this far," Khalid mumbled.

"At least we're alive," Masood said.

"A lot is changing," Ahad added.

"Hey, it's a new life. America should be full of opportunity."

Their conversation ended as a young child, who the three thought to be Bahram's son, came into the room. He held a small tray with some food. *"Salaam,* I thought you could use something to eat after today." He set the tray down on the only table in the room.

"Tashakor," the three men said and the boy returned their smiles before walking out and shutting the door. Khalid, Ahad, and Masood snacked on the bread and tea he had brought in, chatting about old school memories and hoping they could forget the fears that nestled in each of their chests.

IX

January 2, 1980
Peshawar, Pakistan

About a week had passed. Khalid, Masood, and Ahad sat against the wall, Ahad playing with the empty carton of cigarettes he bought in Jalalabad, Masood drifting in and out of sleep, and Khalid picking the grime from underneath his finger nails. The tray of food Bahram's son had brought in the morning lay on the ground, tea glasses drained and plates emptied. Khalid stared at the dishes and ran his hand across his oily face.

"I need a real meal." Khalid stated, his voice fully waking Masood and drawing both friends' gazes. "And a shower." The men had been living in their own filth for days. A thick, sticky smell congested the air. Ahad could barely stand the scent of his own clothes and had considered stripping during the night as the smells of dust, sweat, and oil from the sheets and the clothes kept him from relaxation.

"We need to stay hidden," Masood muttered. Although he tried to oppose, Masood's eyes gave him away. Every one of them craved to leave the house.

"No one knows our faces and it will only be a quick trip."

Ahad wondered if Michael was in Peshawar yet. Michael was Ahad's American friend he met in Kabul who was helping him leave Pakistan. He had no way of communicating with Michael while staying in the house so there was no way of knowing whether or not he was in the city. Before, they had planned that Michael would leave Kabul a week after Ahad left and meet in one of the hotels in Peshawar. Ahad didn't think Michael would be in the city so he wouldn't bother checking. However, Ahad needed to leave the house. The grime felt inescapable.

"Where would we go, though?" Masood asked.

"The main street. We can have a meal and go to the public bathhouse, too." Khalid shrugged. The public bathhouse was a popular edifice around Afghanistan and Pakistan. It was commonly used since most people didn't have access to showers in their own homes. Ahad remembered using it often when he was younger and he longed to feel clean again.

"I could definitely use a scrubbing," Ahad said, grimacing at his own sour breath.

With hesitation, Masood gave in. "Well, I guess that sounds appealing." They were all aware of the risks of leaving. After crossing the border, soldiers could be prowling the streets, searching for their faces to throw back into Afghanistan. And once they were back in Afghanistan, after the news broke that the three had tried crossing the border illegally, they would face the consequences of arrest or death. However, they were desperate.

"It'll be worth it," Khalid said, hitting Masood's shoulder. "It's been too long since we've had a proper meal." Khalid's face lit up with excitement.

After letting Bahram know they were heading out, the men packed their money and left. They walked for a while along the houses, until they turned a street corner with a few *rekshas* along the road. The three hopped into one and were taken into the Peshawar main street which was lined with shops and clouded with cigarette smoke. There was a loud buzz of people shouting and talking as crowds bought fruit and sweets that lined the stands. The air was cool and smelled of cooking meat. Ahad's stomach growled on instinct. He saw chicken *karahi* being eaten by some townspeople, the dish letting off clouds of steam.

"What first, shower or meal?" Khalid asked.

"Shower," Masood said. "We can't go into a shop looking

like we do." Ahad glanced at Masood; his hair was matted, his skin darkened with spots of dirt and oil, his clothes wrinkled and dusty. Khalid looked the same, his eyes swollen and lips chapped. His beard was tangled and had flecks of naan in it. Ahad didn't want to look in a mirror.

They all headed down the road until they came upon the bathhouse, a few people coming in and out, walls echoing with the sounds of water splashing. There was a shop just outside the bathhouse stocked with soaps and shampoos that the three each decided to buy with the money from Hamid and Isah. Ahad still hadn't used his own savings and was trying to salvage the money the men had given him. Luckily, the soaps and travel fees weren't expensive and he had enough of Isah and Hamid's money left over. After the three bought what they needed, they walked into the bathhouse.

The bathhouse was a building open for families who couldn't afford their own bathrooms. Ahad would go there with his father every three or four days at five in the morning when the sun was just beginning to break into the day. It was a sanctuary. Every time he and his father went to the bathhouse, Ahad felt renewed. It was as if his worries were being washed away with the dirt.

Some families would build an outhouse that had a low pressure faucet and a hole in the ground for going to the bathroom. However, it couldn't compare to the fresh feeling after going to the bathhouse. One section of the bathhouse had private rooms with hooks and short shelves for clothing and soap. The lines for these rooms were longer while the other half of the bathhouse was completely open and people would freely wash themselves.

They each took a bucket then went into the back room that held a large pool of hot water. They each filled their buckets and waited for an open room. Once inside, Ahad took off the pair of clothes he had been wearing every day, the nakedness somehow already cleansing, and took a small dish and scooped the water over his body. As soon as had felt the hot water on his skin, his muscles relaxed, enjoying the refreshing splashes. He scrubbed his skin until it tingled, washing all the dirt from his hair and body. The three took over an hour to clean off a week's worth of dirt.

After feeling satisfied, Ahad changed back into his clothes and, although the fabric was still dusty and worn, he felt much better. Ahad left the room to see Khalid outside, combing his beard with his fingers. Masood stood next to him, his face clean and youthful. Ahad himself felt refreshed and ready to take on the day.

They walked out laughing.

"I feel reborn," Masood said.

"That was the best wash I've had in my life," Khalid agreed.

"I'm glad we came." Ahad looked around. The day was bright and crisp and the street was full of appetizing smells. "Where should we eat?"

"Here looks good," Khalid said, leading the two others into a small food shop. They each ordered hefty piles of rice with meat. Ahad took a spicy kind of beef kabob called *chapli* he used to eat in school, and felt elated as he tasted the heat. He would always be grateful for the food Bahram and his wife provided, as well as the risk they were taking to help three fugitives. However, Ahad was glad to finally have a fulfilling meal.

"I've never tasted anything so good in my life," Masood commented, his mouth full of rice. The three young men sat and ate with indulgence, scraping their plates clean of every grain of rice. Khalid leaned back after he took the last bite.

"Oh, man," he let out a long breath. "Didn't I tell you guys this was a good idea?"

Ahad laughed. "I'm clean. I'm full. This was the best idea."

"Isn't there someone you need to meet?" Masood looked at Ahad with his brows up in question, his hand rubbing his bloated stomach.

"His name is Michael. He's helping me leave Pakistan."

"Oh." Masood's voice dropped to a whisper. "Are you leaving now?"

"No, no, I don't think he's in town yet." Ahad was fine laying low for a while. Omar was well-acquainted with Michael and Ann, who was the director of the American Cultural Center. The three of them helped devise a plan for Ahad's trip. By next week Ahad guessed Michael would be in town to join his travels. Later, Ann would fly in to meet with them.

The three continued back to the house. Ahad knew the risk of leaving too early and feared the suspicion it could raise. Soldiers could be searching for him, especially after the stunt he pulled at the border. Ahad rubbed his hand across his choppy hair. When he was a child, he jumped at any chance to get out of the house: playing soccer with his teammates, eating at a friend's house, seeing the kite fights. Now, Ahad was cautious as ever, and although Ahad itched to get to the United States, he knew the chaos needed to settle.

X

1968

Kabul, Afghanistan

Ahad and his father hopped onto a bus to travel to the annual kite fights. It was the end of winter, spring just beginning to break, the trees starting to bud. Ahad sat on the bus next to his father, the wheels whirring against the road, scenic mountains seen from the window. The bus was full of families traveling to the fights, kites in hands, careful not to wrinkle the paper or bend one of the rods.

As the bus pulled up to the stop, Ahad could already see hundreds of kites in the air. He wasn't competing this year but he was determined to run one down. He was never able to catch one before; someone else always grabbed it before him. Outside, the sky was crowded with dozens of different colors and designs. A swarm of oddly shaped birds swimming and diving through the air.

It was early in the morning as Ahad and Qadir walked through the field, faces watching the sky. Kites made from carefully measured bamboo and vibrant paper rippled in the wind. Around, adults whose faces were drooping from age and children who had just begun school came together. It was a celebration of sorts, and everyone from town would come to watch or compete.

Hours dwindled away and Ahad met some friends from school. Late afternoon came. Kites started to drop like birds. Around him, Ahad saw competitors straining their necks. There were two people involved in flying a kite: the person holding the wheel and the kite flyer who held the string with tough leather gloves or finger covers. The flyers all had some sort of protection on their hands. Ahad knew all too well what the thread of kites could do to a flyer's hand. It was sharper than a knife and could cut through skin with one wrong move.

Ahad eyed a particularly stunning kite, with beautiful red paper that dominated the sky. Determined to run it down, Ahad watched. He crouched in a ready position, prepared any second for it to falter. Minutes sped past and soon Ahad's muscles were stiff. Just as he was about to give up he saw it. Another yellow kite approached the red and cut across its thread. The red kite began to plummet.

Ahad burst into a run, his eyes never leaving the turbulent kite. It twisted in the air, turning different directions, leading Ahad away from the other kites. He jumped past adults and children around him. The steps of other kids running it down echoed in his ears. Ahad picked up the pace, his heart racing, his feet taking on a mind of their own.

The kite came closer to the ground. Ahad leapt forward, grabbed hold of it in his hands, careful not to rip the paper, and gathered the thread in his other hand. However, Ahad couldn't see the person to the side of him, who yanked the kite from his grasp. The kite almost left Ahad's hands but he tightened his grip, pulled it back into his possession, and ran.

As he ran he felt a burning sensation running along his fingers. He treaded to a stop and looked at his left hand. Right across the fold of his pinky finger, a deep slash straight to the bone. A fiery pain shot up his forearm. The white of his finger bone was stark against his skin. Mesmerized, Ahad stared as his own blood dripped onto the ground.

He slowly walked back to his father, the crimson kite proudly in his right hand, and his left hand soaked in blood the same color. Qadir's face lit up at the sight of the kite and fell almost immediately as Ahad held out his hand.

A numbness spread over Ahad's skin. The events that happened next were a blur in his memory. Flashes of images scattered his mind. Qadir wrapping cloth around the cut. Rushing home. The bandage soaked with blood. A grin on Ahad's face. A battle wound and a scarlet trophy.

XI
January 13, 1980
Peshawar, Pakistan

After another week or so, Ahad, Khalid, and Masood traveled back to the main Peshawar Street and had a rich meal of hot rice and meat, along with fresh bread. Steam rose from the mound of food and let off hearty and warm aromas. Each bite was just as satisfying as their first meal. Once their plates were scraped clean, Ahad gave them both a look. "I should go find Michael now."

The two nodded. "Where is he staying?" Masood asked.

"The hotel down the street, probably."

Khalid stood. "Alright, let's go." His voice was steady but he knew this might be the last time he would be seeing his friend.

They walked down the road until they came across the hotel. Khalid and Masood waited outside as Ahad walked in and asked for Michael Foster. The man behind the glossy counter told him the room, and Ahad began to weave through the maze of identical hallways until he saw the room number. The sound of his footsteps echoed off of the plain beige walls. He took a deep breath and knocked on the door. A man opened the door, dark skin with dark brown hair, and a familiar smile.

"Ahad!" Michael greeted Ahad. Michael was here to help Ahad leave Pakistan. They had been talking about this long before Ahad ever left and the sight of him made Ahad think of all the challenges to come.

"Michael," Ahad said with a smile.

"Glad to see you in one piece." Michael spoke in English. He was an American teacher in Afghanistan who met Ahad a few years ago. Ahad had been learning English for a while, and would need to be fluent once he was in the United States.

"Yeah, I'm here with two friends." Ahad's accent was thick and each bouncy English syllable felt foreign in his mouth.

"How was it so far?" He gestured for Ahad to come in.

Ahad stepped into the hotel room. "It was tough but I'm here now. What are we going to do next?"

Michael sighed as they both sat. "I need to take you to the Consulate so we can talk to the counselor."

"For what?"

"To see what we need to leave Pakistan."

"When?"

"As soon as possible. When would you be able to?"

Ahad paused. In his mind he had never really left Afghanistan. Peshawar had similar smells and sounds. Steaming rice, fresh bread, the clatter of dishes, the bustle of people. At night he would dream of home and being with his family, but each morning, Ahad would wake up with fear. He needed to leave. He would have to let go of everything he was raised with, his family, his friends, the food. After getting to the United States—*if* he got to the United States—he would have to try and help his family leave. They were depending on him. Ahad knew he had to get this process moving.

"I have everything I need with me now," Ahad said.

"Great, so you can just stay here."

Ahad nodded. "I need to say bye to the others, first." Ahad left the room and walked outside of the hotel where Khalid and Masood stood.

When the two friends saw Ahad, they knew this was goodbye. "It looks like I'm staying at the hotel," Ahad said. It felt strange. The three men stood there, in the cold afternoon air, with nothing but the clothes on their back, staring at the ground. Ahad's mind cut back to his house, the warmth of dinners and each of his family's faces. He saw Omar's grave face, his mother's, his father's. Ahad braced himself for another farewell.

"Alright. I guess this is where we part," Khalid muttered in a flat voice.

"Good luck with everything, Ahad Jan," Masood said. He smiled but Ahad saw nothing but age, exhaustion, and fear in his face. Ahad gave a feeble smile in return. Masood had always been the one to brighten up the mood after a lost soccer game. He would push the teammates around, punch their arms if he saw someone frowning. But now those days were nothing but memories Ahad would carry with him.

"Same to you both," Ahad said and embraced each of his friends.

"*Khodahafez*, brother," Khalid whispered. Despite Khalid's tough exterior, Ahad knew he was the one who had trouble saying goodbye. He could see it in Khalid's drooping eyes.

"Maybe one day our paths will cross again," Masood said, though Ahad doubted the reassurance. It was difficult to imagine the obstacles each would face in the future and when they would ever get a chance to meet again.

"*Khodahafez*," Ahad mumbled and turned away, choking back a wave of sadness as he walked back into the hotel. Instead, he focused on the rhythmic beats of his steps, until all he could feel was his feet on the ground.

XII

January 15, 1980
Peshawar, Pakistan

Ahad stood next to Michael, in front of a squat gate with dark metal bars that blockaded the entrance of the American Consulate. Michael gave Ann's business card to a guard to show the counselor. The counselor Ahad and Michael were meeting with had been in contact with Ann, who asked him to do everything in his power to help Ahad leave Pakistan.

Michael and Ahad waited outside. About ten minutes had passed, although Ahad felt as if he had been waiting for hours, left to stand in the chilled morning air with his spinning thoughts. This was it. All he needed was a visa and he could get out. He tapped his fingers against the back of his hand, steadying his breath and muttering prayers for whatever was about to come next. *"En-sha-Allah."* In God's will. A phrase commonly used to bring good tidings.

The guard finally returned and led the two into the building. They made their way through a few clean hallways then entered an office. Ahad saw a man sitting behind a desk with a fair complexion and a white head of hair, dark glasses resting on his nose. He wore a suit and sat with his hands folded on his desk.

"Counselor Harris, thank you for meeting with us." Michael shook his hand. "This is Ahad. I'm sure you are familiar with his situation."

"Yes, quite familiar. Nice to meet you."

Harris shook Ahad's hand, and Ahad responded in English, "Same to you, sir." Ahad's heartbeat picked up. Since Harris had been in communication with Ann, he was fully aware of how Ahad crossed the border, who he was with, and why he needed to leave. He could easily tell the Afghan military Ahad was there in Pakistan; they would prevent him from ever leaving the country. Ahad's mind throbbed from his racing thoughts. Now that Ahad was in Pakistan with an American, during a time of disorderly politics, he looked more suspicious than ever. But Ann had talked to Harris so there was nothing to worry about. Or that's at least what Ahad told himself as he sat down in front of the counselor.

"So what do we need to do to leave Pakistan?" Michael said, his voice even and controlled.

"Well, first thing is you need a passport so I can get you a visa."

Ahad paused. He had tried to get a passport before but was flatly denied. There were certain requirements one needed to get a passport: military service, education, good political relations. Since Ahad was fresh out of college, had no military experience, and couldn't use sickness as an excuse to leave Kabul to get medical treatment, he wasn't eligible. When Ahad was denied, he had to go through the system and bribe officials to give him the necessary documents. But something went wrong. Someone had found out and Ahad was denied a second time. Ann and her husband, Chris, the Afghan *attache*, had helped Ahad throughout the process, and when it failed, they turned to their only other option: crossing the border. "Um, I don't have it, sir," was all that he could articulate.

"He doesn't have a passport and I don't think he'll be able to get one, either. With the border crossing and all," Michael clarified. They were so caught up in crossing the border that the idea of needing a passport never crossed their minds.

"I'm sorry but I can't help you unless you have a passport." Harris leaned back in his chair.

"How would we get one now? There's no way the Afghan

embassy will allow him to get one after what he did."

Harris paused. "There are plenty of people who can get you one under the radar."

Ahad froze. Surely Harris didn't mean forge one.

"I see," Michael finally said.

"Once you have a passport, then I can help you," Harris repeated. Ahad could have laughed in that moment, but his body was tense. How long would it take him to get a passport? Crossing the border was hard enough, and Ahad's mind still buzzed with the adrenaline from that night.

"Okay, thank you, sir. We'll be in touch. Thank you for your help," Michael said, and gave a quick nod at Harris.

"Thank you," Ahad muttered and he stood. A panic started to build in Ahad's chest as he walked out of the room.

XIII

January 16, 1980
Peshawar, Pakistan

After returning from the Consulate, Ahad asked around for any people who made phony passports. There was a large Afghan population in the town and since Michael couldn't speak Farsi, Ahad was the one talking to the townspeople. Everyone seemed to know the works of the passport business and Ahad's questions never raised suspicion. Ahad was relieved that people were as helpful as they were. Finally, he was able to find the room number of a man who made passports in the hotel down the street.

Ahad and Michael left their room, Ahad wondering how easy it would be to get the passport and how quickly he would be able to get a visa afterwards. He was so close. They walked out of the hotel and got into a *reksha*, travelling until they came across the hotel. Ahad glanced around the main street, a long road packed with hotels, shops, and people. The two men walked into the hotel and through the winding hallways until they finally came across the room number Ahad had found. As they approached the door, Ahad could smell the faint scent of cigarettes.

After giving Ahad a brief glance, Michael knocked. The sound cut through the silence of the hallway. Ahad could hear shuffling behind the door, until they both heard the click of a lock. The door swung open. As Ahad saw the man's face, he froze.

In the doorway right in front of him, Rashad stood, staring at Ahad with those tired eyes. The tired eyes Ahad had always seen growing up. Rashad was a family friend, Qadir's best friend, in fact. He would come over, eat their food, sleep on their furniture, and basically live with them. Then one day, Rashad came and asked to borrow Qadir's most expensive rifle, a sleek, masterful piece that never missed a shot. Ahad's family always practiced generosity. So without a second thought, Qadir handed over the rifle, and Rashad was never seen again. They later discovered that Rashad sold the rifle for twice its worth. Ahad hated him, despised him for betraying his family like that, and now here Ahad was, staring into the face of the same man.

"*Salaam,*" Rashad greeted. Ahad said nothing, and since Michael didn't speak Farsi, there was a pause. Rashad's gaze flicked between the two men. Finally, Michael nudged Ahad, gesturing for him to say something.

"*Salaam,*" Ahad started, "I heard you had a business." Ahad tried to control the rage in his voice and stared at the man before him. Did Rashad remember him? Ahad tried to analyze Rashad's face, searching for any glint of recognition or contempt. Instead he was met with a blank expression, almost bored. It made Ahad's insides knot. Here Ahad was, at the mercy of a man who stole from his family, one who didn't even remember who Ahad was. It was infuriating.

"I see," Rashad muttered and stepped aside to let them inside. Michael walked in but Ahad didn't move, partly out of shock and partly out of spite. Before Rashad could walk away, Ahad spoke in a low voice.

"Rashad, do you remember who I am?" Ahad said through his teeth.

Rashad looked Ahad up and down and brought a hand to his chin. "You look familiar, but no. Where do I know you from?"

"I'm Ahad. Qadir's son." Ahad longed to grab Rashad by the neck and pin him against the wall. To hurt him just like he hurt his father. But Ahad held back; there was too much at risk.

"Oh, Qadir. I remember him." Rashad looked away, as if he

had to search for the name in his mind. "Well, let's get this business done and you can be on your way." Rashad turned into the room where Michael was waiting. Ahad clenched his jaw and followed.

"So you're trying to get out of Pakistan?" Rashad said and sat down in a chair.

"Yes, but I need a passport," Ahad replied.

"You crossed the Afghanistan border, yes?" Rashad continued. "Of course you did. And now you can't go back to the embassy." There was amusement in his voice. Ahad masked all of his anger and fear behind an unmoving expression. Rashad's nonchalance made Ahad's head throb with resentment. How could Rashad not even care? Not even recognize him? After all of the hate and disbelief with which his family was left, here Rashad was, right in front of him, and Ahad couldn't do a thing without risking something going wrong.

"So will you help us?" Ahad asked.

"Only if you can pay."

"How much?"

Rashad paused and looked around the room, pretending as if he were calculating important numbers. "750 dollars."

Ahad's jaws dropped. That was the entirety of Ahad's savings. It was like Rashad knew exactly how much money Ahad brought over. Rashad sat there with a sneering grin as thoughts raced through Ahad's head. After stealing from and leeching off Ahad's family for years, Rashad was doing it again, and Ahad had no other choice but to hand over the money. Ahad gave Michael an astonished look. "750." Ahad translated. Michael's eyebrows drew up in shock. Ahad knew there was nothing else that he was able to do.

"Yes, we can pay." Ahad's voice was deflated. The defeat he felt was overwhelmingly heavy and he wondered whether it was even worth it to leave Pakistan. There went Ahad's savings.

"Perfect." Rashad glanced between the two men. "Of course, you'll need to fill in some papers and take photos and all that technical business. I need to get stamps and everything to make it look official, so you should come back in a few days."

"Fine." Ahad turned and stormed out of the hotel room. Michael followed him into the hallway and shut the door.

"Ahad, what happened?" Michael jogged to catch up to Ahad and grabbed his shoulder. "Is it the money because I can help ou--?"

"No, it's not the money. It's the man who wants the money." Ahad grimaced and tried to control his breathing. He needed to calm down.

"What about him? Yeah, he seemed a little pretentious, but what other choice do we have?"

Ahad silently debated whether to tell Michael what was really going on. He paused, searching for the right words. He could barely find what he needed to say in Farsi, let alone English. "He stole from my father and used us so he could have food and a place to live." Michael frowned and shook his head.

"Man, that's awful. No wonder he's in this kind of business. It suits him." Although comforted by Michael's words, Ahad couldn't push away the image of Rashad's smug face. Michael and Ahad were just as involved in this process. They needed a passport and they had no other choice but to stoop to Rashad's level. "But we just have to do what we need to do," Michael said and patted Ahad's shoulder as they walked along the street.

Ahad sighed. "You're right."

XIV
January 19, 1980
Peshawar, Pakistan

Ahad and Michael now stood at the door of Rashad's hotel room. Over the past two days they both were laying low, taking a break from all of this refugee madness. Ahad spent his time praying for his safety and health, thanking Allah for getting him this far. He realized Rashad was testing Ahad's self-control, his pride. Ahad knew no matter how much he wanted to get revenge, he had gotten too far to let his temper get the better of him.

"Are you ready?" Michael looked over to Ahad who nodded and knocked on the door. When Rashad opened the door, Ahad felt all of his old anger rush to his face again. He took a deep breath.

"*Salaam*, we were wondering if the passports were ready," Ahad said, careful to keep a level voice. Rashad gave that smile that made Ahad feel sick and stepped aside to let them both in.

"So," Rashad began, "you're going to need to fill in all of your information." He gestured to the small table, which had a dark blue passport booklet with gold lettering on the cover. "I'm also going to need you to take your photo down the street because I don't have a camera." Ahad nodded and sat down to begin working. On the table there was also a note from the Office of Afghan Refugees permitting Ahad to leave Afghanistan.

For the next hour or so, Ahad filled out the passport as Rashad sat to the side and pulled out a cigarette. Ahad could feel the anger rising to his head. The passport didn't even look official. Ahad could easily tell the difference from a real Afghan passport. The misprints of words, the ink smudging. He almost said something but decided against it, knowing God had put him in this situation for a reason. Plus, they would have to wait a long time before finding another person who did this type of business.

"I'm done," Ahad said and put the pen down.

"Okay, now go take your picture and come back. I'll fill in the stamps." Rashad stood from his chair and grabbed the ink pad and stamp, which Ahad could see carved into a potato. As Ahad and Michael walked out of the room, he couldn't believe he was paying $750 for this. For Rashad to stamp a messy passport with a potato. However, Ahad did what he was told and left the room.

Michael and Ahad walked along the street, down towards the shops where a photo place was tucked in between two restaurants. People buzzed along the shops, in and out of restaurants. Ahad could smell the tangy turnip scents cloud the air as they walked past. Turning into the shop, Ahad reflected on how grateful he was for his friend's company. Although Michael couldn't do much, with the language barriers and all, it was comforting to have his friend there with him each step of the way.

"*Salaam,*" Ahad said to the man behind the counter. He had a thick beard and a turban wrapped around his head. "Could I have my photo taken?" The man led him into the back of the shop and Ahad sat against a gray wall while the man picked up a large fancy camera. Ahad's mustache was still thick under his nose and his hair had grown out just a little bit since he had cut it. He adjusted the wide collar of his shirt and looked into the camera.

The man removed the lens cover of the camera for a few seconds then recovered it. He then disappeared into another room to develop the image. When he came back he held a small photo in his hand. "Okay that's it," the man said. Then he handed it to Ahad. After giving the man a small fee, Ahad and Michael walked out of the shop, comforted with the knowledge that this process would soon be over.

XV
January 24, 1980
Peshawar, Pakistan

Ahad and Michael sat in Counselor Harris's office again as Harris looked over the messy passport. Both Michael and Ahad held their breath. This was the determining factor to whether or not Ahad would get to leave and time was running out. Ahad was sure that the Afghan military was getting suspicious at this point; there were probably soldiers strolling along the streets of Kabul and near the American Cultural Center, to see if Ahad would show his face. Finally, after a few minutes, Harris spoke.

"Well, I'm not entirely sure what an Afghan passport looks like," Harris paused and Ahad swallowed a wave of nausea, "but it looks good to me. There are stamps and signatures so you're good to go." Michael exhaled and let out a small laugh of relief. "I'll take it to one of my colleagues now." Harris stood and left the room.

"We did it," Michael whispered in disbelief. He was beaming. Ahad looked over at Michael and saw a wide grin across his face. Ahad couldn't help but reciprocate. After a few minutes, Harris walked back into the office and handed the passport back to Ahad. Opening it, Ahad looked at the muted ink of the visa. It felt like a dream.

"You'll also need to do a few more things to ensure a smooth travel," Harris said. "To leave the country you have to go see a doctor and get all your vaccinations. After that, you can get your flights."

"Thank you, sir."

"Is there anything else we should keep in mind as we move forward?" Michael asked.

"Well, you need to figure out exactly how you'll be getting to the United States. You need to see a travel agency for the tickets but it might be best to go to Islamabad because there are more options there. Talk to Ann about the whole situation. I would wire the American Cultural Center to let her know you're ready to leave."

"Thank you, again, sir." Ahad shook Harris's hand, Michael following in suit, and they walked out of the building. Looking at the visa again, Ahad noticed the scrawled English words. April 24, 1980. It was valid for three months. For some reason that date felt comforting. A tangible day. Everything that has happened up to this point felt like a dream to Ahad; now, he could see himself in the United States. He could see the cities of America. He could see himself on the streets. After looking at so many photographs, whispering plans with Omar, he was so close. His moment of relief was quickly swept away by memories of his family. This was about more than him. He had to keep that in mind.

XVI
January 26, 1980
Peshawar, Pakistan

Ahad and Michael took a taxi to the Peshawar airport. After calling the American Cultural Center, they talked to Ann who found a flight to Pakistan. It was the afternoon when her plane came in. When Ann walked outside and saw Ahad and Michael she smiled. "Ahad, it's so good to see you." She gave Ahad and Michael each a hug and her presence washed over them like the warmth from a fire. It was nice to see a familiar face. She reminded Ahad of his sisters, and over the past few months she had become just like one to Ahad.

Since she was the Director of the American Cultural Center and her husband, Chris, was the Afghan *attache*, she was the person in the best position to help Ahad. She understood his position; she knew how to work through the political system; she was the tie between the United States and Kabul. Ahad's worries were overwhelmed by his gratefulness to see her.

"You too, Ann," Ahad said. With tears in her eye, she turned to Michael and gave him a hug, thanking him for being there to help move things along.

"You've been such a big help," she said, looking up at him with her big smiling eyes.

"I'm glad I could help a friend out." Michael glanced over at Ahad. In this moment, Ahad felt like he was home for the first time in months. He realized how much hate and tension had been spreading through Afghanistan, how much deceit and unfaithfulness he saw. But here he was, knowing how lucky he was to have his two friends with him in these trying times.

"Let's go to my hotel so we can talk," Ann said, and the

three traveled back to Ann's hotel. Once they arrived, they walked through the hotel entrance and took the stairs to go two floors up. Once they got to her room, Ann let them in, and the two men found places to sit. Ann's eyes were shadowed with dark circles but her smile showed the genuine happiness she felt to see her friend again. She was anxious to hear the whole story of how Ahad made it to Pakistan.

"So, I see you got to Peshawar okay," Ann commented to Ahad once she had closed and locked the door.

"It wasn't easy but I'm here now. Have you organized your trip to the United States?"

"About to. I'll need to find tickets to California. My dad is sick in the hospital and my mom is with him now. Have either of you done anything?"

"We're trying," Michael replied.

"We need to buy plane tickets," Ahad added.

"Okay, I see. Well, I'm headed to Islamabad since most planes pass through that airport. You'll find better travel agencies there to get tickets."

"That would be great." Ahad felt like he was back in Afghanistan.

"So, tell me what happened to you, Ahad. I haven't seen you since that day at the Cultural Center." Ann sat down and let Ahad and Michael tell her about all the troubles he had gone through these past few months. With each story, Ann's eyes grew wider. The three talked for hours. Ann was aware of the difficulties he had faced but they both knew there were many more ahead. The minutes sped by as they caught up with each other's lives.

"I think we should organize our trip out of Peshawar," Ann said after listening to Ahad. "It's not safe here. There's no international airport in Peshawar so we'll need to travel to

Islamabad. I won't be able to fly with you guys because I have to go from Islamabad to Los Angeles."

"Is everything alright?" Michael asked.

"He has cancer. He's in the hospital now."

"I'm so sorry. I hope it all works out," Michael said in a soft voice. Ahad gave a similar reassurance.

"Thank you both. But after you get to New York, you can call me and we can decide what to do from there. Once you're in the United States, there'll be a whole other process to go through with citizenship and immigration papers."

Ahad swallowed the lump in his throat. How would he ever be able to get through all of this? It might be months, maybe even years, before he was able to settle down again. He felt a pang of nostalgia for his family. The only thing he wanted to do in that moment was go home to his bed and eat a hearty dinner. But he pushed those thoughts aside. He couldn't torture himself like that.

Soon, it was midnight. After hours of talking, Ahad found out that Americans evacuated Kabul because of the Russian invasion. Chris, Ann's husband, would be flying to the United States in a few days. Ahad and Michael left to go back to their own hotel room and Ahad thought about the plane tickets they would need to buy. He used all of his money on the passport so there was no way he could pay for his own ticket. However, he found out Qadir had given Michael some money before Ahad left for Peshawar. With that money, Michael covered the expenses. Ahad missed his family and wished he could be back home, hunting with Qadir. But there was no way Ahad could go back. He tried to think optimistically and hoped he could go hunting once he was in the United States. That night, Ahad's dreams were filled with memories of his family.

XVII
January 27, 1980
Islamabad, Pakistan

The flight to Islamabad was nerve-wracking. Ann showed Michael and Ahad the travel agency she used at the Peshawar airport and Ann bought their tickets. Once the tickets were taken care of, it was only an hour before boarding the plane.

Peshawar didn't feel that different from Kabul. The crowded streets, the food vendors, the smells of cardamom in the air. But as Ahad boarded the plane, he knew he might never be surrounded by his own rich culture again. Islamabad wouldn't be a huge jump from his hometown either, but who knew what the United States would be like? Ahad had a feeling Americans didn't have markets full of *jelabi* and *nuqul* lining the streets during Eid. His mind spun from worry but he tried to focus on the present.

Ahad had never been in a plane before. Although excited, he felt fear churn in his stomach. He didn't know what to expect. After waiting for the flight, he, Ann, and Michael made their way through the gates and walked outside to board. Ahad noticed how small the plane was. It was a twenty-passenger aircraft. He walked up the stairs to the door of the plane and found a seat in the cramped space. Still no luggage. He only had a small pack of old clothes. In Peshawar, Ann had bought him a jacket, a shirt, and a new pair of pants. They couldn't buy anything more until they were out of Pakistan since they were tight on money and the clothes were expensive.

As Ahad sat down, he felt strange. There was this feeling he couldn't shake off. He knew that this was it. He had his visa and was on a plane. After this short flight, he would be in Islamabad and ready to board the next plane to fly to the United States and leave behind the culture he was so familiar with.

When the plane started to move, Ahad felt his stomach lurch. The plane flew at altitudes that made the landscape below look miniscule. However, Ahad could still see the contrast of Islamabad. The entire manicured city looked like it resided in a completely different country. The height made Ahad feel nauseous so he closed his eyes. When they arrived in Islamabad, Ahad took a deep breath. Definitely not as bad as he thought.

Ahad, Michael, and Ann walked into the Islamabad airport. It was much bigger than the one in Peshawar and each gate buzzed with crowds of people: Americans, Afghans, Pakistanis. Ahad felt reassured. Here, he could blend in and slip through, unnoticed, just another traveler.

After arriving, the three traveled around the capital to see the historic. They saw ruins of rocks and stones, scattered across stretches of land. As they traveled, Islamabad looked like a city from the west. It had paved roads, trees, large houses full of wealthy people, and new cars driving down the streets. There were barely any *rekshas* in sight, and shops and restaurants were neatly placed along the town. It was completely different from Kabul and Ahad already felt thrown into a new culture.

However, Ahad's fears subsided. Now there was a way out of the mess he had gotten himself into. Although a discomforting thought came to mind. Ahad was moving farther from his family while Ann was going home. He knew his actions weren't in vain. By leaving he would separate his family from his own personal issues with the government. They wouldn't need to help Ahad escape the military's advances and end up getting caught. However, Ahad still felt as though he were abandoning them. His family still knew of his destination and soldiers could be questioning them at that moment.

But Ahad tried to focus on spending time with his two

friends while he could. Ann was leaving the next day and Ahad didn't know when their next meeting would be. He prayed for her safety and health because she was like family and had helped Ahad navigate the messy politics of Pakistan. She knew about Ahad's issues with the military, knew about his need to leave. She had kept his plan secret and helped him get to Islamabad, all while worrying about getting to her own family. He truly admired her for that kind of selflessness.

The day faded and the three made their way back to the bustling airport. They took a taxi across the back to the airport and walked to the entrance. "Alright, I guess it's time for me to leave." Ann's mouth pressed into a soft smile. "Thank you again for being there and helping with this whole ordeal," Ann said to Michael with a grin. They both embraced and Michael smiled back at her.

"No worries, Ann. Safe travels, I hope your father gets well." Michael nodded at Ann and Ahad, stepping away to give the two friends some space.

Ahad and Ann were left in private to speak. "Thank you," Ahad said.

"I'm glad I could help. You've had a long trip, Ahad."

He laughed. "Well, it's not over yet."

Ann smiled again. "I wish I could stay longer and travel with you. I hope you can forgive me for leaving you behind but I have a feeling we'll see each other soon. You just worry about getting to the States safely." She always had that friendly warmth. Everyone at the American Cultural Center back in Kabul felt safe with her; they could tell her anything. And her loyalty proved invaluable when Ahad needed it.

"I wish you the best," Ahad said. They hugged and Ann turned to leave, giving Ahad one last wave before disappearing inside the airport. She slipped past the crowded lines, flashing the black color of her passport to show her status as a diplomat. Ahad wished it could be that easy for him.

Ahad turned and walked away with Michael, thinking about the events to come. They would find their flights with one of the travel agencies around Islamabad the next day, and from there, Ahad would travel to the United States. The evening was cool as Michael and Ahad made their way to dinner. The streets were still. Once they were back in the hotel room, Ahad felt closer than ever to his new life and he wondered what it would feel like being in the United States.

XVIII
January 28, 1980
Islamabad, Pakistan

After mapping out all of their options, Ahad and Michael finally found a flight to the United States. From Islamabad they would fly to Karachi, Pakistan, then to Athens, Greece, then to Amsterdam, Netherlands, then to London, England, and finally to New York. Each of their tickets was a little over one thousand dollars and Michael covered Ahad's expenses with a bankcard. There were no words to tell Michael how much the gesture meant to Ahad. The flight was set to leave in a week.

Once the flights were sorted out, it felt as if most of the stress was lifted off their shoulders. No more tricky expenses. No more sneaking around. All they had to do now was get on a few flights. And why not enjoy the journey? Since the layovers left the two with time to kill, they planned to go to the England embassy.

They sat in the office of the embassy, attempting to arrange a visa for London, so they could explore for the few hours they had in the city. Ahad never left Afghanistan, and now he had the opportunity to explore cities of which he had only seen photos. He was young, able to speak some English, and eager to start a new life. This was his chance to be a tourist instead of a refugee.

The man who sat before them had a small plaque on his desk displaying his name on a bright gold plate. Joshua R. West. "Hello, Mr. West." Michael extended his hand and Ahad did the same.

"Please take a seat." West gestured to the two chairs in front of them. "So, what can I do for you both?" He was young, pale, with dark curly hair. His accent sounded strange to Ahad.

"Well, we're leaving Pakistan, and we have a few flight layovers including one in London. So we were hoping we could get a visa for the day and go sightseeing."

"Okay. I'll need to see your passport, then."

Ahad handed it over. As West took it and started flipping through, a doubt crept into Ahad's mind. He tried to reassure himself. Harris had approved of the passport, so surely West would do the same. West paused while looking at one of the pages.

"Where did you get this passport?" West asked.

"My embassy, sir." Ahad's heart started to race.

"Is there something wrong, sir?" Michael asked.

"Well," West lowered the passport so Michael and Ahad could see, "the stamps here look a little smudged." He pointed to the bright purple ink next to Ahad's photo. "I'm going to have to call the Afghanistan Embassy just to make sure everything here is valid."

"Oh, okay, no problem, sir." Michael's voice got very quiet, and he leaned back in his chair. Now, Ahad's heart pounded. He tried to catch Michael's eye, but Michael only stared at West as he dialed the number of the Afghanistan embassy into the blocky rotary phone. Ahad cursed silently. How could they be so careless? Their flight was less than a week away. They had gotten this far and if West gave the Afghanistan Embassy Ahad's information, well, that would be it.

Ahad wanted to interrupt, to take back the request for a visa, but there was no way Ahad could say anything without looking suspicious. The ringing echoed from the phone. *Ringing.* Ahad couldn't breathe. *Ringing. Click.*

"Hm, it's not connecting. We can try this later," West said, hanging up the phone.

"Oh, it's completely fine, sir," Michael said and choked out a nervous laugh.

"While we wait, why don't I ask you both a few questions so I can better understand this situation?"

"Sounds like a good idea." Michael folded his hands.

"So, why are you both leaving?" West stared with narrowed eyes. All of a sudden, he wasn't as nice as he'd first appeared.

"Well, I've always wanted to travel to the United States and around England. And Michael has told me so much so I wanted to go and see it on my own. It'll only be a visit," Ahad said, trying to control the shaking in his voice.

West nodded, eyeing Ahad's passport again. "How long have you two known each other?"

"About two or three years," Michael responded. The questions went on like this for about an hour. West tried calling the embassy three or four times, each time not connecting through or cutting off with a busy signal.

As the last attempted call ended, West sighed and shook his head. "Well, I can't get through. They're probably very busy today." Then West stood. "Wait here. I'm going to get my supervisor to see if there's anything we can do." West walked around the desk and out of the office with Ahad's passport still in hand.

Ahad looked at Michael. This was a mistake. Ahad didn't dare whisper but the two shared the same worries. What if West confiscated the passport? What if Ahad was stuck here? About fifteen minutes had passed before West walked back into the room. He strode to his chair and, without sitting, threw Ahad's passport onto the desk.

"We can't offer you a visa so don't come back here again." West's gaze pierced through Ahad, who numbly grabbed the passport and nodded.

"Thank you, sir," Ahad muttered before leaving the room in

a daze.

They both walked out, hearts racing, knowing they would not be coming back.

XIX
February 2, 1980
Islamabad, Pakistan

Michael and Ahad avoided more trouble and knew that in a matter of a few days, they would be out of Pakistan. Ahad couldn't wait to have the government out of his hair. He couldn't wait until he could walk the streets without worries of arrest. He went to a doctor in Islamabad to get vaccinations, and he was given a packet that verified Ahad as a healthy passenger. On the day of their flight, they woke up at sunrise, took showers, and prepared for the uncertainty ahead. Once they checked out of the hotel, they traveled back to the Islamabad airport.

Ahad couldn't believe it was already time to get ready to leave. He wondered how this week of rest and relaxation could end so quickly while the weeks he had waited in hiding felt like years. After everything he had been through, it somehow all seemed surreal. Moments blended together and if he mulled over his experiences, it felt like remembering a dream.

As Ahad and Michael walked into the airport, Ahad was only carrying a small bag of a t-shirt, pants, socks, and underwear. Michael held an extra pair of Ahad's clothes in his own suitcase, the original pair he was given the first night Hamid and Isah came to his house. Ahad wanted to throw them away, but Michael refused. For some reason, he found sentiment in the dark fabric. Ahad guessed Michael was parting with another part of his life as well.

They walked through the airport entrance to the passport checkpoints. Although Ahad knew these were there before, only then did a fear run through his mind. Anyone in this airport could be someone from Afghanistan, a representative, a government official. One look at Ahad's passport, and he would be sent straight to jail. His flight was leaving in four hours. He had to make it through.

Ahad stood in line for one of the booths and tried to control the shaking in his hands and ran through prayers in his head. Once he got to the booth, he handed over the passport and paperwork, watching the man's dark eyes scan it. Ahad's heart was pounding and he prayed. He should have been more prepared. What would he do if the man looked up at him and told him no? What if Rashad turned him in? He could have easily taken Ahad's money and told someone Ahad was a fugitive. Rashad was that type of man. But after a minute, the man stamped his passport and handed it back to wave him through. Stepping away, Ahad exhaled deeply, and his heart slowed again.

As Ahad walked farther into the airport with Michael by his side, an immense weight lifted off of his shoulders. Now all they had to do was wait. Ahad felt as if he had just come up from underwater. The relief flooded into his chest like a breath of air. Everything seemed brighter. And for a second, he didn't feel tied down to Afghanistan anymore. However, as soon as that thought crossed his mind, nostalgia hit him in the face like a soccer ball.

He would always be tied to Afghanistan. Its dirt roads, its rich smells, its stunning scenery: mountains, lakes, fields. He may always be connected to his hometown but he couldn't let himself be dragged down by nostalgia. He needed to hold himself accountable for his own decision to leave. It was either sacrificing his home, his life in Kabul, or letting himself and his family be at the risk of arrest in the hands of the government. He had no choice. He cursed himself for forgetting what this trip was truly about. He couldn't be selfish. Not at that moment. After everything his friends had given up. After leaving his family in a state of chaos.

Ahad and Michael waited on the second floor. At the gate a few rows over, Ahad saw a few Afghan men, and thought they looked familiar. They could have been from the border. Ahad dropped his head and tried to remain calm and nonchalant, but his heart was raging. Each small movement or whisper from the men made his insides knot. He suddenly felt nauseous.

Each minute that passed was complete agony. Anyone who walked past them could have been a threat. Anyone there could expose Ahad for what he was doing and take him straight back to Afghanistan. He could barely keep up a conversation with Michael. He thought the sound of his voice would make the men notice who he was, even though Ahad wasn't even sure who those men were. He thought over every possible scenario that could have happened before he got onto the plane.

Ahad could be spotted, arrested, taken to jail. The plane could be stopped. Ahad and Michael could be searched and Michael could be charged for association with a criminal. Maybe they would arrest Ahad's family, find Ann and Chris. Arrest anyone who had helped. Ahad's head throbbed.

Finally, the time had come to board. Even as Ahad walked through the gate and then outside to the plane itself, he felt anxious. There was a restlessness he couldn't control and he folded his hands, his fingers tapping mindless rhythms on the back of the other hand. The plane was much more massive than the first one he had taken in Peshawar and heightened Ahad's worries. More passengers meant more chances someone could stop Ahad.

He looked for his row and sat down. Scanning each face that appeared through the plane door, Ahad tried to relax. Once everyone had boarded, the plane began to move.

Ahad's nerves were still unsettled and he prayed as the plane got into position. When it came to a stop, Ahad assumed the worst. Maybe someone had seen him. At any second someone could burst through the doors and drag Ahad off the plane. Only as the plane accelerated across the concrete runway did Ahad relax.

Now he knew he would make it through. He took this time to reflect and think about how far he had come. His mind wandered to the early days of his childhood. He could smell the scents of *bolani* wafting through his house on those long summer days. The rich smell of dough swelling in the kitchen. He remembered buying *baklava* along the streets of Kabul and he already missed the taste of the pistachio. He missed the fresh days outside and the family memories he used to make.

XX

1967

Kabul, Afghanistan

Ahad and his father, Qadir arrived in northern Afghanistan. They were there for two reasons: a friend, Muhammed, had reached out and said there was a pair of swans spotted at a nearby lake. These massive birds had some of the richest flavor and Ahad and Qadir jumped at any chance to bring some home.

Muhammed was also lent a black Arabian stallion bred for the King's son. As soon as Ahad laid his eyes on this horse, he was overcome by awe. It was stunning in color: a sleek, groomed black that had a glossy sheen. Its body was muscular and Ahad could tell only the most privileged, most wealthy families would ever ride it. How Muhammed was ever able to get the horse bewildered Ahad, but he didn't dare question it as if the creature would vanish in front of his eyes.

Qadir brought his best German shotgun to pin those swans. Hunting was something Ahad always looked forward to with his father. Since Ahad was the oldest of his siblings, he always took hunting trips with Qadir. His chest would swell with pride whenever he caught a goose or duck.

Qadir, Muhammed, and Ahad squatted behind layers of bushes and plants, the horse secured behind them. The sun rose over the lake, the light reflecting on its lapping waters. The graceful silhouettes of two swans at the water's edge came into view. Qadir balanced his gun, aiming the barrel straight to the swan. Leaves and twigs obscured part of Ahad's vision. His heart was racing. Everything around Ahad was so still, so quiet. The suspense made Ahad hold his breath. The crack of a gunshot. The wounded, horn-like scream from one of the creatures.

The swans came racing with wings outstretched towards them. Fear pounded in Ahad's head and he couldn't bring himself to close his eyes as the swans soared directly at their faces. Only feathers away from Ahad's face, they swooped up and launched themselves into the air.

Qadir and Muhammed had already stood. Muhammed mounted the tall hors and pulled Ahad to sit behind him, who gripped onto Muhammed's waist. The air whizzed past Ahad as they spurred into a gallop. Ahead of them, the swans flapped side by side. Ahad could see one struggling in the air. All of a sudden, the two swans split and Muhammed guided the horse to follow the wounded one. After a few minutes of chasing and bouncing on the horse's back, the swan fell onto an open plain ahead of them. There, another hunter stood watching.

The hunter scrambled over to the swan and started to pick it up. Then another gunshot cracked in the air. The hunter flinched, the ground next to him spraying up chunks of grass and dirt. Muhammed held the gun straight at the man, the barrel still smoking. The hunter's face flooded with fear as he realized he had two choices: leave the swan or get shot. So he fled.

After Muhammed brought the horse around to the swan, he slowed to a stop and hopped off to help Ahad to the ground. Muhammed picked up the swan and dropped it in front of Ahad to see. Ahad let his eyes scale every feather of that massive bird.

It lay on its back and its wings were outspread in a crooked angle. Blood stained its pure white chest. A thin rib bone was exposed to the air. Ahad looked up at Muhammed who smiled and folded his arms as he stood above the fallen beast.

That swan would feed both his own and Muhammed's family for a week. The meat would be cooked with rice or made into a thick sauce with potatoes. Ahad bent down to measure the swan from beak to tail with his hands.

In Afghanistan, this is how everyone would measure. Ahad's pinky on the tip of the bird's beak, the thumb down towards its neck, his hand fully outstretched. Careful not to lift his thumb, Ahad brought his pinky to the spot his thumb reached and then reached his thumb down the bird again. On and on with his young, small hands all the way down the bird. Fifteen hands long. With an adult's hand like Muhammed's it still would have reached an impressive eleven or twelve.

Ahad, though only a bystander in the hunt, still felt a touch of power. There he was, having ridden a royal horse with something as mighty as a swan resting at his feet. There was something in that moment that seemed like a dream. In that moment, a promise was made. Ahad promised himself that once he was older he would buy his own gun, a quality one like his father's, and befall something as big as—or, if Ahad dared to imagine, something bigger than—this bird. Whether or not that day would ever come, Ahad had no idea.

XXI
February 2, 1980
Amsterdam, Netherlands

Ahad was exhausted. He and Michael were now about half way through their layovers and had gotten off the plane in Amsterdam. This airport was much larger than the Islamabad airport and Ahad felt as if he would be walking for hours just to get out the front doors. Although, since he didn't have a visa to explore Amsterdam, he and Michael would have to wait in the airport for the next eight hours.

Maybe it was their restlessness, their exhaustion, or perhaps the newfound sense of security and safety after finally leaving Pakistan, but for some reason, Ahad and Michael both wanted to get out. So, they asked a security guard if there was an immigration office in the airport so they could get a one day visa to explore Amsterdam. After being directed, they made their way to the office. It didn't worry Ahad as it did in Islamabad. The distance between him and Kabul made him feel more willing to take a risk. So, they both walked past gates and shops until they found the immigration office.

As they approached the area to which they were directed, they saw a man with blond hair sitting behind a squat desk. The space was surrounded by tall glass panels to section it off from the rest of the airport.

"Hello, sir. My name is Michael and this is my friend Ahad. We were wondering if it were possible to issue a visa for today so we can explore Amsterdam while we wait for our next flight."

"Where are you both flying to?"

"London, sir," Ahad replied.

"He's a tourist and heading to America and since we'll be

waiting for the next eight hours for our flight we thought we might make the most of it." Michael gave a charming smile.

The man paused. Ahad noticed a nameplate on his desk: Louis Abbes. "Okay, can you both give me your passports?" Abbes stood and held out his hand. The two gave over their passports and Abbes walked to the corner of the room where a door led into another section of the office. "You two can wait here." And after a quick knock, he disappeared, shutting the door behind him. Ahad looked over at Michael, who shook his head to reassure that it would be fine.

About ten minutes had passed before Abbes emerged again, and he came out with another person. The other man held Ahad's passport in his hand and Ahad felt a buzz of fear run through his body like electricity. He regretted coming into the office.

"Mr. Faieq, where did you get this passport?"

Ahad swallowed the lump in his throat. "The passport office in Afghanistan, sir."

"And where are you going? Why are you leaving Afghanistan?"

"We're going to the United States, sir. We're tourists and we just wanted a visa to explore Amsterdam while we wait for our next flight," Michael cut in.

The man paused and handed the passport back to Abbes, giving a suspicious look. Without another word, the man walked back over to the door and disappeared into his own office. Abbes looked at the two men and gestured for them to stand. He gave their passports back, and Ahad's hands were trembling.

Without a word, Abbes led them out of the office back to the waiting area near the London gate. He turned to them both and pointed to the seats. "You are going to sit here and wait until your plane arrives. I don't want to see you wandering or doing anything else." Then Abbes lowered his hand and with one last glare, walked away. Michael and Ahad sat and waited for a few minutes until they were sure Abbes was nowhere near them. Ahad's breath was shallow and he craved a smoke.

"Do you think he knew?" Ahad whispered. The airport was strangely silent in the late hours of the night.

"They were gone for ten minutes. They could have been talking about anything," Michael responded. They both paused until Michael spoke again. "I mean, the passport was in Farsi. They probably couldn't understand it."

There was another beat of silence. And then, Ahad let out a nervous laugh. Michael grinned. "Why did we even try to do this again?" Ahad looked over at his friend.

"Hey, we thought the Dutch would be different." And the two sat letting out soft laughter as they waited in their seats for the next eight hours.

XXII

February 3, 1980
New York, New York

In the plane, Ahad saw a large span of sleek gray buildings in the landscape. Skyscrapers were at every street corner, cars sped down the paved roads. When the plane landed at the John F. Kennedy Airport, Ahad could barely fathom the size of the building. They walked through wide, brightly lit hallways. It was late afternoon, around three, and Ahad felt exhausted. He had never traveled in planes before and being on so many flights for hours at a time really took a toll, but at least the exhaustion drowned out his worries of home. The only thing his mind had the energy to focus on was the present.

As Ahad and Michael walked in the hallways, the passengers began to approach security. Ahad glanced at Michael, who was wearing a soft gray hat, a *chitrali*, people wore in Pakistan. Michael, barely moving his lips, whispered, "Let's split up." Ahad slowed his pace as Michael walked ahead. They went into two different lines and Ahad held his passport in his hand along with the letter Chris wrote that claimed Ahad was only visiting the United States and described his political involvement with Chris and Ann. It would help Ahad pass through without many questions. They also left their phone numbers to show Ahad didn't forge the document.

As Ahad got to the front of the line he walked up to a light haired guard standing behind the small booth. Ahad gave a polite smile as he handed over his passport and letter. The man grabbed it and glanced through them.

Without looking up, the man spoke. "So what is the reason for your visit?"

"Just a tourist, sir," Ahad said in English.

"Are you carrying anything?" This time the man glanced up at Ahad's small pack of clothes.

"Just some extra clothes." Michael was carrying Ahad's other pair of clothes so it appeared as if Ahad was just a tourist quickly visiting the country.

Ahad answered the questions with ease since he had been asked the same exact things so many times during this trip. Finally, he was here, in New York. The United States. After months of trouble and planning, Ahad was finally where he needed to be. The realization hit him as the man asked a few more routine questions. A genuine smile came to Ahad's face as he took back his passport and letter and was passed through. Since he was so tired before, he barely noticed where he was.

The JFK airport was huge. What Michael had described hadn't come close to what the setting was really like. Natural light spilled in through the windows and there were hundreds of people bustling in and out of security lines and waiting areas. Ahad glanced back at the security lines and saw no sign of Michael. Thinking Michael would be waiting somewhere farther, Ahad continued to walk down the airport, keeping an eye out for sign of his friend.

Ahad walked by a few open doors that led into different offices. As Ahad glanced into one, he saw Michael sitting in a chair across from an empty desk. Ahad approached and Michael, seeing Ahad, snapped his head to check another door in the corner of the room. Ahad was about to speak but Michael waved him away and shook his head. A flicker of fear ran through Ahad's chest and he stepped away, leaving Michael in the office. Panic throbbed in his head as he mindlessly continued forward and got to baggage claim. Here, he would wait for Michael. After finding a bench, Ahad sat and prayed. It would be unfair if

Michael were to get in trouble after helping Ahad with so much.

About an hour had passed before Ahad saw Michael walk into the baggage claim area. Ahad stood, anxious to hear what had happened. Michael stormed towards his friend, yanking on his coat with a grimace.

"What happened?" Ahad whispered.

Michael muttered a few undecipherable curses before actually speaking. "They searched me because of that hat."

Ahad's eyes dropped to the Pakistani hat in Michael's hand. "Drugs?"

"They certainly thought so. Opium and hashish. Had to take off my clothes and everything."

Ahad didn't know what to say. Michael's bag was half zipped and a small piece of clothing stuck out from the top. Ahad assumed they saw the pair of clothes Michael was holding onto as well, but he knew Michael wouldn't tell him that.

"It's already getting late. Let's go. We don't have a lot of daylight," Michael said, still shaking his head in disbelief. They made their way out of the airport and hopped into a taxi. Michael told the driver to go to Manhattan, and as the taxi began to drive away, Michael closed his eyes to rest. The drive was short and Ahad gazed through the window at the mesmerizing city around him.

The buildings were huge, and the streets were crowded with people. There were still shops and food stands, though the food looked completely different. Once the driver finally got to Manhattan, Ahad could see the water bordering part of the city. Michael gave the driver a small fee and they climbed out.

Ahad was greeted with greasy smells of food and the loud hum of people and cars. Michael looked around. "I need a drink." Ahad could see he was still frustrated from the incident at the airport. It was already starting to get dark as Ahad and

Michael walked a few blocks to find a bar and went inside. The room was dimly lit and cluttered with the noises of clinking glass and footsteps. Ahad and Michael both ordered drinks and let the warmth of the alcohol wash over them. They chatted and laughed for an hour or two before feeling the edge of hunger.

Michael finished off his second beer and put down the bottle with a clink. "So what do you want as your first American meal?"

"I don't even know what they have here."

They left the bar in search of a restaurant. The sky was dark and hazy, the air dim from the light of restaurants and shops pouring into the street. Bright signs cast red and blue streams of light onto the bright yellow taxis. As they walked, they passed McDonald's, a name Ahad recognized. This was always what Ahad imagined American food to be like.

Michael saw Ahad looking at the sign. "How 'bout an old fashioned American cheeseburger." Seeing Ahad wander around the streets and looking at the buildings and the people was like watching a child exploring a new place. Ahad was experiencing the American culture to which Michael had grown accustomed.

They walked into the McDonald's. Smells of grease and beef met Ahad's nose, a strange smell compared to the foods at home. The restaurant was glowing with fluorescents and everything felt like it was tinted yellow. There was a long counter at the front, which Ahad and Michael approached.

"Could we have two cheeseburger meals, please?"

"Fries and a drink?" The woman said.

"Yes. Coke please."

Michael handed over a card and the woman swiped it in the register. Ahad wished he had money to pay for some of the meals and travel fees but he had nothing to give.

"So, what do you think of Manhattan?" Michael asked as they stepped to the side.

"It's so different," Ahad said, glancing out the McDonald's door. "A lot bigger than I thought."

Michael nodded in agreement. "The cities here are huge."

"Two cheeseburger meals," a voice called, placing a white paper bag and two Styrofoam cups on the counter. Michael turned and grabbed the bag, handing one of the drinks to Ahad and then sat down at a table. Opening the paper bag, Michael handed what Ahad assumed to be a cheeseburger, wrapped neatly in paper.

"I can't wait to see how you react," Michael said, watching Ahad reveal the burger. Its bun was a flushed beige, and the meat dark, piled with lettuce, tomato, onions, and cheese. Michael's eyes were glued to Ahad, who picked up the burger, hands fumbling to keep all the toppings contained. Glancing up at his friend, Ahad laughed and opened his mouth for a bite.

It was nothing like Ahad was expecting. It was more salty than anything else and grease coated the roof of his mouth. Although his own family cooked with plenty of oils and fats so it didn't bother him. Ahad chewed the mouthful and swallowed.

"It's okay," Ahad said with a shrug. Michael laughed in response and unwrapped his own burger.

The two sat and ate for a while, satisfying the hunger that was making their stomachs rumble, until Ahad and Michael sat back in their seats, hands over their stomachs.

"Is this what all American food is like?" Ahad asked.

Michael shrugged. "I don't know, there's a lot of stuff but this is most accessible." Michael crumpled up the trash, ready to get up. "We should call Ann."

"Good idea."

"There are phone booths around the street we can use."

After throwing away their trash, Michael and Ahad left the McDonald's. The streets of Manhattan were still busy, and a gust of wind brushed against Ahad as he stepped out. The two walked a block or so to get to the nearest phone booth, a tall, skinny structure. Ahad stepped in first, pulling out the scrap of paper Ann had given him, looking at her scrawled phone number.

Since the phone was a collect call, Michael showed how Ahad first had to connect to an operator and then give the number. Once Ahad heard the voice of the operator, he said Ann's number as clearly as he could. And the phone began to ring.

"Hello?" Ann's voice sounded scratchy through the receiver.

"Hi, Ann, it's Ahad."

"Hey, Ahad. It's good to hear from you. How was the trip?"

"It went well, we're in Manhattan now. We arrived a few hours ago."

"Did you run into any issues?"

Ahad paused, and glanced at Michael, who stood in the doorway. "Nothing that gave us too much trouble."

"Okay, well, you guys still need to leave New York. It's expensive there and it'll be easier to lay low somewhere else so try and find a flight tonight."

Ahad suppressed a sigh. He knew he should leave, but he was so worn down from all the travelling. All he wanted to do was lay in his bed back home and go to sleep.

"You can either go with Michael back to Phoenix or somewhere else, but do whatever you can to leave," Ann said after hearing Ahad's silence. At this point, Ahad didn't bother prodding Ann with questions. He knew she was more capable to navigate the situation and make sure Ahad didn't end up in an unwanted situation.

"Okay, we'll head back to the airport now." Michael glanced up when he heard Ahad.

Ahad quickly said his goodbyes to Ann and hung up.

"We need to leave?" Michael asked.

Ahad nodded. "Do we have anywhere to go?"

"We can try and see if there are flights for Phoenix."

Michael and Ahad walked out of the phone booth and hailed a bright yellow taxi. They climbed in, Michael telling the driver to go back to the JFK airport. The drive felt shorter on the way back and in about an hour, they arrived, paid the fee, and hopped out of the car.

They made their way through the massive airport until they got to the airline counter to ask a woman who was working.

"Excuse me, when is your closest flight to Phoenix?" Michael asked. The woman scanned her computer screen before speaking.

"The next one is February fifth for $800." Michael raised his eyebrows and looked over to Ahad. They had an unspoken understanding. Too long of a wait and way too much money.

"Okay, thank you, ma'am." Michael smiled and the two stepped away from the counter. "So now what are we going to do? Get on a random flight?" They stood in silence for a moment before an idea came to Ahad.

"Actually, a few years ago, one of my friends gave me his phone number. He told me he was going to Nashville."

"Nashville?"

"Yeah, but I'm not sure if he is still staying there."

"It's worth a shot."

"Is it too late to call?" Ahad asked. It was nearing midnight and Michael bit his lip.

"It might be, yeah." He paused. "Do you want to check flights anyway?"

Ahad nodded and they made their way back to the ticket counter. Michael ended up buying a flight to Nashville for about 300 dollars that was leaving in a few hours. It wasn't too expensive and it was fast enough to get out of New York. Also, they needed to go somewhere, and even if Ahad's friend wasn't there, Ahad and Michael could find a hotel. So they sat at the gate, nodding off in the waiting area, listening for the flight's announcement of departure.

XXIII
February 4, 1980
Nashville, Tennessee

Ahad stood, dialing the number of his friend, Saleem. Ahad and Michael were in Nashville now. They barely slept on the flight, and felt the fatigue and jetlag of all of their travels. The novelty of flying wore off on Ahad, and the trip blended together with the dozen others he had taken in the past couple weeks. It was about six in the morning, and Ahad was hungry again, but he knew he only had to endure a bit longer before all of this would be over.

The phone began to ring. *Click.* "Hello?" Saleem's voice was deeper than Ahad remembered, but it still brought a smile to Ahad's face.

"*Salaam*, Saleem Jan, it's Ahad. From soccer." Ahad greeted in Farsi. They had played on their school soccer team together back in Afghanistan. Saleem left for the United States instead of going to college. Ahad tried to remember. Was it five years since he had last seen Saleem? Six?

"Ahad Jan! *Salaam!*" Saleem exclaimed. "It's so good to hear from you! How have you been?" The two fell comfortably back into their native language.

"Good. I've recently left Afghanistan with my friend Michael and we're in the Nashville airport right now."

"Wow, Ahad, there's so much we need to catch up on. I'll come down and pick you up right now. Hang in there. You both can stay at my house and have a good meal."

"*Tashakor*," Ahad said and they quickly bade goodbyes.

"So I assume he's here?" Michael grinned.

"Yes, and he's coming over to pick us up right now." Ahad

was thrilled to be able to see one of his old friends again. He was already starting to feel disconnected from his life back in Afghanistan and seeing Saleem would help give Ahad a little bit of comfort. Just hearing his voice made him feel like he was back home.

After a few minutes, Saleem came to pick Ahad and Michael up, greeting his old friend with an embrace. Ahad introduced Michael and they climbed back into his car, ready to head somewhere they could talk freely. Saleem's girlfriend was also in the car, and they exchanged names.

"Ahad, Michael, this is Lina."

"Nice to meet you. Thank you for coming to pick us up," Ahad said.

"Oh, it's no problem at all." She was an American girl, very beautiful with sleek brown hair and hazel eyes. Once they arrived at Saleem's apartment building, they went up to his place and gathered in the kitchen. There, Saleem and Lina began to make breakfast for the two. The welcoming nature of Saleem reminded Ahad of the community feeling back in Kabul. Neighbors were always friends and families would open their doors to complete strangers. Saleem's kindness dampened Ahad's stress of being a foreigner.

"So, how was the trip?" Saleem asked them both in English.

"Difficult," Ahad responded.

Michael laughed. "But we got through it in one piece."

They ate their breakfast of eggs and toast, Ahad grateful for Saleem's kind welcome. Michael's eyes were already drooping so he slept on the couch. Lina disappeared somewhere in the apartment while Ahad sat with Saleem in one of the two bedrooms.

"So, tell me how you've been all these years, Ahad Jan." Saleem spoke in Farsi, and Ahad felt like he was back in high school.

"It's a lot to tell, and I still need to hear what happened to you," Ahad said. They began to tell each other everything. Soon, six entire hours had passed. Ahad's throat was sore from talking and laughing with his old friend and his eyes felt swollen and heavy. Saleem could see the exhaustion on his face.

"You need to sleep." Saleem stood to let Ahad sleep in the room in which they were talking. "You can rest in here for as long as you need." Saleem gave Ahad a warming smile. Ahad would have protested but he could barely form the words. Every part of his body felt twice its normal weight. So Ahad gladly accepted Saleem's offer and returned the smile.

"*Tashakor.*" Ahad waited until Saleem left the room and collapsed on the bed, falling into a deep sleep and not stirring until many hours later.

XXIV
1970
Kabul, Afghanistan

Ahad and Musa were very close friends. Musa and his father, Habib, would come to visit Ahad's family often, and would always bike over. Their bikes were glossy and beautiful and every time they visited, Ahad begged Habib and Qadir to let him ride Musa's bike. Ahad never had a chance to ride Qadir's bike, because it was much too big for him.

One day, Qadir came home while Ahad was sitting in his room after school, and called Ahad outside. Ahad stopped in the middle of his schoolwork and made his way to the front of the house where his father stood with a brand new, glossy bike. Ahad's mouth dropped, rushing over, hesitating before touching the bike. One of the newest bike models in Kabul. Ahad could hardly believe it was in front of him.

Ahad must have spit out *"Tashakor"* a thousand times before even taking it from his father's hands. All of his schoolwork was abandoned to ride down the street. He spotted a friend of his, Abdullah, who also owned a bike and planned to bike in the mountains together the next morning.

Ahad went home and was barely able to sleep. His mind kept coming back to the fantasies of riding his bike around the city. Now, he didn't need to ask to ride Musa's bike when he visited. Dawn came. 5AM. It was time for Ahad and Abdullah's trip. Ahad had been awake every second of the night. Since neither of the boys had school, they planned to take a long ride into the park a few kilometers away and ride the bikes into the winding paths up the mountain.

Ahad scurried outside and grabbed his bike and after riding

down the street to meet Abdullah, they began their journey. Ahad's new bike was alarmingly fast. They sped through the town and soon got to the entrance of the park, Abdullah a couple meters ahead of him, leading Ahad through the trail.

Ahad was too excited to notice the ache in his legs. Adrenaline overpowered him, giving him bursts of energy. The trail was surrounded by beautiful, old trees with branches that extended over top of them like a roof. Soon, Ahad and Abdullah were biking the trails into the mountain. Ahad's adrenaline began to wear off. He felt as if he were pedaling through sand. His breath became quick and shallow and soon Ahad regretted not getting sleep the night before.

Minutes sped by. Ahad was just about to collapse. Then the incline released into a quick downhill trail which relieved Ahad of pedaling. The bikes picked up speed, Ahad's stomach lurching from the acceleration. Abdullah turned a corner. Gaining momentum, Ahad sped behind. As he whizzed around the corner, Ahad was closer to Abdullah's bike than he thought. In an instant, Ahad shut his eyes. His body lifted from the seat. His hands slipped from the handles. His back hit the ground. Ahad let out a loud grunt and lay still. It took a moment to process what had just happened. Abdullah had also fallen but it was more of a stumble for him, so he stood and helped Ahad up.

"Are you okay?" Abdullah's eyes were filled with fear.

"I'm fine." Ahad rubbed his face. His body ached. "But how's my bike?" Ahad looked past Abdullah's shoulder to see his new bike laying on the ground. He rushed over and his jaw dropped. The entire front wheel was bent. Tears burned in his eyes.

There was no way that Ahad just destroyed his new bike. As Ahad tried to lift it up, the bike was unable to stand. Abdullah stood quietly watching as Ahad tried to tend to the bike's injuries.

After a few minutes of trying in vain to fix the casualty, Ahad stood. "We're going to have to take it back."

Abdullah nodded and in a gentle voice he said, "I'm sorry, Ahad."

Without saying a word, the two boys found a way to grab Abdullah's bike and drag Ahad's all the way back home. On the walk back, Ahad felt every muscle in his body burn; his legs were weak; a bruise was forming on his back where he had hit the ground; and the effects of the sleepless night were taking a toll.

Ahad dreaded to hear what his father would say. However, it was exactly what Ahad expected. Qadir was furious. He shouted and muttered curses as he examined the wheel. After the amount of money his father had spent, Ahad gladly took Qadir's words as punishment. He continued about how Ahad wouldn't be getting a bike after this and he wouldn't be riding out anymore and Ahad could only hang his head in shame.

After a few weeks, however, Qadir brought back the bike as if it were brand new. The wheel was replaced at the local bike shop in town. Ahad didn't dare let himself get excited this time around but he was still overwhelmed with gratitude. He thought he would never see this bike again. But there it was, propped up in front of him, graceful, sleek, and ready for the next ride.

XXV
February 5, 1980
Nashville, Tennessee

Ahad woke up the next morning, feeling replenished with energy. He stood from Saleem's bed and rubbed his face. As Ahad walked down to the kitchen, a wave of thankfulness washed over him. He was lucky to have both Michael and Saleem here to help him. Allah had truly blessed him with these people.

Upon entering the brightly lit kitchen, Ahad saw Michael drinking a cup of coffee as Lina and Saleem bustled around to make breakfast.

"Good morning, Ahad." Lina smiled. "Sleep well?"

"Yes, I did. Thank you." Ahad gave Lina a kind nod and stood at the kitchen entrance.

Saleem, noticing Ahad's politeness, quickly gestured him in. "Please, take a seat, we have breakfast covered."

"*Tashakor.*" Ahad sat in a chair at the end of the table. The room smelled of steaming coffee and citrus. Ahad wondered what kind of fruits they would usually eat in the United States. Dried melon didn't seem like a popular option. Saleem brought Ahad a large cup of tea. It smelled differently from the tea back home and the steam carried floral tones to Ahad's face.

"Ahad," Michael began, and took a sip of his coffee. "I found a flight to Phoenix and I'll be leaving soon. But I think it'd be best for us to travel separately so it seems less suspicious." Even through everything Michael had done for Ahad, he knew Ahad was capable enough to handle himself.

"That makes sense." Ahad nodded. "I can fly out to you after a few days, a week, maybe."

"You can stay here as long as you need," Saleem offered.

"*Tashakor*, but I won't need to stay long. I can organize a flight later."

"And while you stay we can show you around Nashville," Lina suggested with an excited grin.

"Sounds great." Ahad smiled and they all continued on with a peaceful breakfast, chatting about old memories and new beginnings.

Later, Ahad stood outside Saleem's house as Michael was ready to depart. This goodbye didn't feel as pressing since Ahad knew he would be seeing Michael in a number of days. So, with a quick hug and a pat on the back, Michael was set to leave.

"I'll see you soon, Ahad. Here's my address and other information if you need to reach me. You can come down whenever you're ready."

"Thanks, Michael, I'll see you soon." Michael jumped into the taxi that was waiting on the side of the road. As the car pulled away from the curb and disappeared into the distance, Ahad took a moment to take notice of the area around him. The air was just as cold as in Kabul, which bewildered Ahad, and there was fresh snow on the ground. Diners and shops were visible down the road. Clouds drifted across the gray sky and the houses around him were colored a dull beige. The air smelled fresh and crisp and the roads were completely flat and paved. Ahad missed the dirt roads of his childhood and the hours he spent under the blue Kabul sky.

With a quick sigh, Ahad turned and walked back into Saleem's house, brushing away the nostalgia. Instead, Ahad thanked God for getting him here, where there weren't soldiers on street corners, ready to take him away in cars. The town of his childhood was gone. Ahad reminded himself there was only danger and trouble left in Kabul, and there was no use to dwell on what had already passed. His father taught him that. The past should remain in the past. So Ahad pushed away the memories and closed the door to Saleem's house.

XXVI
February 12, 1980
Nashville, Tennessee

The past week was full of sightseeing. Saleem took Ahad all over Nashville—to different museums and parks. The weather was cool but the parks were still bright and green. There weren't any flowers in bloom, but Ahad could still see the small buds. They also went to plenty of restaurants, trying all kinds of food. Before parting, Michael and Ann gave Ahad money which he used to cover his meal expenses. Ahad became particularly familiar with what Saleem called "comfort food," of fried meats and creamy rich side plates. Saleem would also cook Afghan food which helped Ahad settle into the foreign city.

Ahad became better acquainted with Lina, as well. Ahad thought Saleem and Lina worked well as a couple. She was always so positive and full of conversation. Saleem had always been the talkative type back in high school and Ahad barely saw him upset or angry. Just like Lina, Saleem was always beaming, and Ahad couldn't have been happier for his old friend.

When the time came to leave, Ahad readied himself for his flight to Phoenix. He bought the flight with the money from Michael and Ann with plenty still left over. He carried his small pack that he had taken with him on every flight which held his other pair of clothes. Ahad stood at the entrance of the airport, facing Saleem and Lina. They both smiled, though there was a sadness in their eyes. Ahad braced himself for yet another goodbye. Even though Afghanistan was thousands of kilometers away, Ahad still felt like he was parting with home.

"Thank you, both. For everything," Ahad said. His words almost disappeared in the gentle breeze. Ahad slipped into

English, as a polite gesture to Lina.

"Same to you, Ahad. I felt like I was a high schooler again." Saleem laughed and they both shook hands and pulled each other into a hug, then kissed each other's cheeks three times as friends and family would do in Afghanistan.

After pulling away from Saleem, Ahad turned to Lina. "It was so nice to meet you."

"You, too, Ahad. I'm glad I could meet one of Saleem's old friends from back home." She smiled sweetly, and pulled Ahad into a hug.

"Fly safely and keep in touch."

"I will. Don't worry." Ahad gave a final nod to each as he stepped away and waved. As Ahad turned his back on them, he inhaled deeply. The air smelled earthy like it had the day he left Kabul. The days seemed to be passing more quickly than ever and he still needed to send a letter back home to tell his family where he was now. Ahad was still terrified of what his future held and what was to come of his family. Fear became second nature to him. His dreams were filled with the echoes of gunshots, the sound of blood dripping onto the floor, his family's faded voices. Each day was another hazy filter over his memories and he became less and less familiar with the faces of his family. He felt more separated than ever from them.

Even as Ahad boarded his flight to Phoenix, he could barely think of anything else. Even though he left Kabul, was his family really safe from those who were looking for Ahad? They still had his name, knowledge of where he was going and Ahad realized he would need to find a way to get his family out of Kabul. There was no telling what the soldiers would do to find Ahad. Knowing his disappearance from Kabul was the most suspicious thing he could have done, Ahad's mind pounded with guilt for the entire flight.

XXVII
February 12, 1980
Phoenix, Arizona

The plane touched down onto the runway and Ahad stirred from a sleep he didn't realize he fell into. With the droning sounds of the wind against the wings, the plane slowed to a stop and Ahad blinked away the sleepiness sticking to his eyes. At the airport, Michael would be waiting for Ahad, so he hurried off the plane to greet his friend.

Ahad walked through the Phoenix airport which was full of people. The windows let in the soft, afternoon light, illuminating the glossy white floors. Making his way out of the building, he saw Michael inside a white car and hopped in.

"Hey, how you doing, Ahad?" Michael greeted him as Ahad shut the door and buckled the seatbelt.

"Great. Tired of travelling, though. You?"

"Yeah, it never really stops. But I'm good, it's nice to see my family again." Michael pulled away from the curb and drove out of the airport.

"Will I get to meet them?" Ahad put his bag near his feet and leaned back into the chair.

"Oh, absolutely. You'll be staying with all of us, actually." Michael grinned upon seeing Ahad's raised eyebrows. "They're a fun group, don't worry about it."

"Thanks for all of this again, Michael." Ahad laughed. With a wave of a hand, Michael brushed off Ahad's words. The two sat and chatted about their weeks and what they had been up to. After some time, they arrived at Michael's house. It was a modest one story home with warm toned walls and a dark roof. Michael parked and led Ahad inside.

The inside of the home was full of color and warmth. Ahad saw three women sitting in the living room, whom Ahad assumed to be Michael's mother and two sisters. They were all very dignified in appearance, the daughters taking after their mother's eyes and smile. Ahad also noticed Michael had the exact same smile.

"Ahad, this is my mother Joan and my two sisters, Alicia and Nicole."

"Nice to meet you." Ahad smiled at the three ladies and shook their hands. "Thank you for letting me stay with you."

"Oh, no problem at all. Please stay as long as you need to." Joan smiled at Ahad, who felt eternally grateful to Michael and his family. Michael had shown him the utmost hospitality and treated Ahad like a brother.

Back in Kabul, he was always taking care of his siblings and providing for the family when he could. As the oldest sibling, he had to shoulder some responsibility. So this entire trip pushed him out of his comfort zone since he was the one receiving help instead of giving it. Everything Michael had done made Ahad feel guilty because he couldn't do anything to repay him. But Ahad shook those thoughts out of his mind and focused on the present.

XXIII
February 15, 1980
Phoenix, Arizona

Ahad settled into Michael's home with hesitation, eventually allowing himself to accept the Fosters' kind offer. The past few days were restful, busy only with the outings Ahad and Michael would take. Michael showed Ahad the city, the best places to eat, and the best places to hang out with friends. Joan was so kind towards Ahad, and the sisters were both strong-willed and funny. It was a completely different family dynamic than his own back home.

Michael had also decided to introduce Ahad to his group of friends. Ahad was getting ready to leave with Michael to a casual restaurant so Ahad could be introduced to the group. Ahad's nerves weren't settled by any of Michael's reassurances. Ahad was friends with Americans back home at the American Cultural Center, so he couldn't understand why he was so nervous. Maybe it was because of the new setting, a different place with which he wasn't familiar, or maybe it was the idea of being an immigrant. Back in Afghanistan, there were only the select few Westerners who came in, but here, in Phoenix, Ahad was the stranger.

Nevertheless, Ahad set his worries aside and drove with Michael over to the gathering. Ahad walked into the restaurant and smelled the now familiar smells of burgers and fries. Ahad wondered what else was on the menu as Michael led Ahad through a sea of tables and chairs over to a group sitting at a round table by the window. The place was well lit with a buzz of people and chatter coming from every table. As the two approached, the five friends looked over to Ahad.

One girl stood up to greet Michael. She had a warm olive skin tone with dark curly hair and dark eyes. The rest of Michael's friends followed her in standing.

As Michael pulled away from the embrace, he grabbed Ahad's shoulder. "Ahad, these are my very good friends, Caroline, James, Matt, Heather, and Jordan."

Caroline, the girl who hugged Michael, extended her hand to Ahad. "I'm so glad I could finally meet you, Ahad. We've all heard a lot about you."

Ahad shook her hand and smiled. He looked around at the table and exchanged polite greetings with everyone. James was a tall man, with rich, dark skin and glasses framing his face. His voice was so deep, Ahad could barely hear him over the restaurant's clatter. Matt was just as tall, though fair in complexion, with brown messy hair and a shadowed jaw. Heather was tan with sleek, dark hair, and bright eyes. Beside her, Jordan, who had hazel eyes and slightly lighter skin than Michael, greeted Ahad and offered a seat.

The group all sat down at the table and handed Michael and Ahad menus. After a quick glance, and a few suggestions for Ahad, they all knew their orders.

Caroline was the first to address Ahad. "So, Ahad, how are you liking Phoenix?"

"It's so nice here. Everyone seems very friendly and Michael's been giving me the inside look at life around here," Ahad said.

Heather took the leap and asked the question on everyone's mind. "So you're from Afghanistan? I heard so much from Michael about the food and the culture there. How was your trip?"

Ahad felt a pang of sadness in his chest but cleared his throat and spoke anyway. "Yes, I am. It's a really beautiful country. And my trip here was crazy. It's a really long story."

When no one spoke, Ahad took the cue to continue speaking. He explained his entire trip and how he left Kabul. Although it was difficult to talk about, it helped Ahad have a stronger sense of closure.

When Ahad finished, the group all wore shocked expressions. "Well, glad you made it in one piece," James said with a smile and raised his water glass as an echo of affirmation passed around the friends. A few hours passed as they all ate and drank a bit, sharing stories and getting to know Ahad better. They were all so kind and reminded Ahad a lot of the friends he made back at the American Cultural Center. Ahad's nerves dissipated and he let himself enjoy the night. He liked every single one of Michael's friends and could see why he hung out with all of them.

Once the night ended, Michael took Ahad home and bid goodbyes to his friends. Though Ahad knew he would see the group again. The night was glowing from the bright yellow streetlights and Ahad sank into his guest bed, mind stirring from the carefree, pleasant night that had passed.

In the following weeks, the group invited Ahad and Michael out to dinner, to tour Phoenix, and to see a movie—the first one he saw in America: John Travolta's *Saturday Night Fever*. It made Ahad laugh. Here was an actor popular among Americans, slick black hair, greasy with hair gel, paired with a bright white suit. Back in Kabul he would always go to the movies with friends to watch old western classics with actors like Charles Bronson and Clint Eastwood. The night with Michael's group reminded Ahad of his days back home and put him in a good mood. To feel in place in such a strange and new setting was comforting and Ahad's stress from the past few months eased with the experiences with his new friends.

XXIX
February 23, 1980
Phoenix, Arizona

Ahad ran his hands along his neatly ironed shirt. Straightening out the sleeves, he looked into the mirror. His hair had grown out again, his mustache bushy, and scruff shadowing his jaw. He was getting ready to go on a date with an American girl set up by Joan. It was embarrassing, really, to be set up by his friend's mother, with a girl of whom he could barely remember the name—Sarah? Cindy?—but Ahad felt as though he had no choice. Joan was adamant about her decision. Once she had her mind set on something, she was determined to see it through.

Ahad glanced one more time in the mirror and sighed. There really was no use to even seeing this girl since Ahad would soon be leaving to D.C. He had a brief phone call with Ann, and she would be coming to D.C. in March to meet Ahad and work out his residency in the United States.

Nevertheless, Ahad left the room and traveled down to a Chinese restaurant down the street. Michael had lent Ahad some money to pay for the meal.

When he got to the restaurant, he saw the girl Joan had described. She was lean with a small build and curly dark hair. Her eyes were a light brown and when she saw Ahad, her face lit up with a smile.

"Hi. Ahad, right?" She approached him. Her voice was delicate and soft; Ahad could barely hear her over the chatter of the other customers. He returned the smile and nodded. He didn't want to greet her, frankly, because he couldn't remember her name. Luckily, she said it for him. "I'm Sandra, nice to meet you!" she chirped.

The two moved into the restaurant and sat at a table. They began to talk lightly about Ahad's stay in Arizona and his experiences in America. Sandra was attentive and kept the conversation flowing seamlessly. Ahad wondered how she could be so naturally social. Compared to his interactions with Michael's group, Sandra talked as though she had known Ahad for years.

Soon enough, their meals were brought over. Sandra had ordered a shrimp dish with noodles for Ahad and a rice dish for herself. When the plate was placed in front of him, the first thing he noticed was the smell. It was salty and pungent. He suppressed a gag. Next, he noticed the actual shrimp. Ahad never had shrimp in Afghanistan and what he saw was much different than what he expected. There, small curled pink and white lumps sat on top of noodles. This is what Americans called meat?

"Let me know what you think!" Sandra commented as she started to cut into her own food. Ahad glanced up at her and nodded apprehensively. Taking a deep breath, Ahad picked up his fork and began to dig in. Sandra showed him how to take the tails off of the shrimp and when Ahad took a bite of his meal, he cringed at the taste. This had to be one of the most disgusting foods Ahad had ever eaten.

Sandra looked up at him. "Don't like it?"

"Not at all," Ahad said and laughed.

"Oh no. I'm so sorry. I really thought you would like it." Sandra covered her face sheepishly.

Ahad laughed it off and began to talk about the food back at home. He just wasn't accustomed to seafood.

A wave of nostalgia crashed into him as he finished. He missed the food back in Kabul. The lamb and kabob lining the busy street. He missed the sweet smells of *jelabi*. The tastes of *bolani* and *ash*, the spices, the savory flavors of turmeric and onion. The *reshteh* was so much better than the bland noodles of his shrimp pasta dish.

As the date came to a close, Sandra paid for the meals as an apology for Ahad's awful dish. After parting, Ahad traveled back to Michael's house. When he walked in, Joan immediately asked, "How did it go?"

Ahad took off his coat. "I hate shrimp." Joan began to laugh and Ahad couldn't help but crack a smile. After quickly thanking her for setting up the date, Ahad went up to his room, ready to brush his teeth and get rid of the lingering taste of shrimp.

XXX
1966
Kabul, Afghanistan

After *Ramadan*, the holy month of fasting, the glorious three days of Eid had finally arrived. The weather was warm and the streets were full of people. Ahad sat in his house, glad to be at home instead of in school. The first morning of Eid was bright and clear and Ahad and his family traveled to the public bathhouse.

The bathhouse was packed. Families from all over the city crowded together to wait for their turn to wash and cleanse themselves. It was a tradition most families practiced during Eid and an aspect Ahad looked forward to every year. Once a space was available, Ahad's family took turns to wash. When it was Ahad's turn, he reveled in the process. The water was hot and Ahad scrubbed his skin, his face, and his hair, until he felt like a snake who had shed its skin. Once clean and dried off, Ahad changed into the fresh pair of clothes his parents had bought him. New attire was another tradition Ahad's family had adopted. The cloth felt soft and pure against his skin and everything in turn felt more crisp and alive.

After bathing, the family traveled back to the house, ready for the day's activities to unfold. At their home, Ahad was met with piles of cookies and different sweets like *jelabi*, a flour and sugar mixture fried to crystallized rings, *nuqul*, sugar coated almonds, and an assortment of roasted chickpeas. Neighbors traveled between houses, exchanging these foods. A few neighbors came over to Ahad's house and the families gathered around on the carpet with mugs of steaming black tea infused with cardamom. The *jelabi* melted on Ahad's tongue, the sticky sugar lingering on the top of his mouth.

To Ahad's dismay, Eid always ended too quickly. Days sped by as Ahad and his friends played soccer outside, ate dinners with each other's families. The marketplace hummed with life. Families set up stands to sell toys and candies they had made days prior. Qadir always gave money to Ahad and his siblings to spend.

Ahad was busy every hour of the day: cooking, playing soccer, eating the sweet and savory foods prepared by neighbors, walking around the marketplace, admiring the vibrant tapestries, the pastel colored candies, the glossy *jelabi*. He woke up to see the sunrise, sunlight melting across the road like liquid gold. The air was swollen from the smells of spicy lamb, the soft aromas of bread.

The three days of Eid would always float in Ahad's mind and memories from Eid made Ahad's chest flutter like a bird's wings. Laughter was always in the air and schoolwork had been forgotten until the new week had started. Everything about those days felt surreal. It left Ahad dizzy with glee. He hung onto each sacred moment of Eid and prayed. Prayed for the health of those around him. For the feeling of Eid to last him through the year. For Allah's light with each sunrise.

After the last day came to a close and the sun dipped back under the horizon, Ahad slept. The night was still and Ahad's dreams were filled with the warm streams of sunlight, the airy laughter of his friends, and the calm rhythm of his own heartbeat.

XXXI
March 27, 1980
Phoenix, Arizona

Ahad stood at the Phoenix airport, suitcase in hand. Ahad still had money from Ann which had paid for the cost of the plane ticket. Ahad had also gotten rid of the small pack he had dragged around on flights. When he was in Phoenix, he bought new clothes and he now had enough to pack a very small suitcase. It was one Michael gave him, a structured gray duffel Ahad could easily shoulder. As Ahad stood facing Michael and Joan and the sisters he had learned to call family, the goodbye felt final. It was as if Ahad was leaving Kabul again. In Michael's face, he saw the same bittersweet smile that Omar wore when they parted. Ahad swallowed the sadness that knotted in his throat.

Ahad spoke first to break the silence that was heavy in the air around them. "Thank you." Ahad could barely find the words. "For everything. You don't have any idea how grateful I am for all that you have done."

Joan smiled and pulled Ahad into a hug. "Don't act like this is the last time I'll see you. Once you get settled in D.C., you better call us. I've gotten used to having you around." She laughed and Ahad couldn't help but crack a smile.

"I will," he assured her. He hugged the sisters and the women walked away, leaving Ahad and Michael to bid their farewells.

At first, neither could speak. They stood in silence watching the bustle inside the airport and hearing the whir of planes on the runway. There was really no way to thank Michael for what he had done. Everything from Kabul to Phoenix was so immensely selfless, Ahad couldn't have asked for a more considerate man to have as his friend through it all. Michael helped Ahad feel at home in a city in which he couldn't even dream of living. Now, Ahad was filled with doubts as to whether he would ever see Michael again.

Although he was in the United States, he had barely made his place here. He still needed a work permit, a citizenship, and he needed to find a way to protect his own family back in Kabul or bring them over which was exactly why Ahad was going to Washington D.C. There he could finalize his residency and move towards a more stable future. Ann and Chris had a house in D.C.; however, they were leasing it out to families while they were in Afghanistan. So they were renting a home on MacArthur Boulevard for the time being until the lease ended for the other residents. Ahad pushed away his thoughts and looked at his friend.

Finally, Ahad spoke. "Thank you, Michael."

Michael laughed, though it was dry and half-hearted. "I've heard enough thank yous these past few months, Ahad." The two friends turned to each other and hugged, slapping each other on the back.

"If there is any way I can repay you, I will." Ahad knew Michael would deny his offer.

Michael shook his head as Ahad expected. "All I need from you is to keep in touch. I know the next few months will be crazy and you have a lot ahead of you, but my mom was right. I was getting used to having you around." They both laughed. Michael glanced at his watch. "You better go. You still need to get through security." His voice was soft.

Ahad nodded and steeled himself with a deep breath. There was nothing Ahad could do. He had to push away the sadness of another goodbye and move on. That was the only way to make sure Ahad wouldn't be stuck reminiscing on what had already passed. He heard his father's words in his mind. *What is done is done. You can only move forward and learn.* So Ahad looked up at his friend, one he would never forget, and said, "*Khodahafez*, Michael Jan."

Michael smiled at Ahad's words in Farsi. To the best of his ability, Michael returned the farewell, with his plain American accent. They both laughed and Ahad finally stepped away, turning his back on Michael, his family, and Phoenix, a place he had learned to feel at home in, and walked towards yet another flight and yet another change.

XXXII
March 27, 1980
Washington D.C.

Ahad got off the plane in the early afternoon. He had spent the flight suppressing waves of memories from Kabul and Phoenix and tried to focus on the prayers he muttered under his breath. As he walked through the arrival gates, Ahad spotted Ann, who had a grin spread across her face. Ahad walked up to her with a smile and hugged her.

"Nice to see you!" Ann said.

"Same to you," Ahad said.

"Can't wait to hear about your time in America so far," Ann said and Ahad let out a laugh.

Together the two went off to Ann's car, and drove to the small rental house off of MacArthur Boulevard. As they drove, Ahad let his mind wander to the possibilities awaiting him in D.C. Maybe Ahad could study and reaffirm his place in the U.S. It was an idea he had to discuss with Ann, but Ahad was excited about the idea of moving forward. He had gotten a bachelor's degree at University of Kabul for Mechanical Engineering. Although, Ahad was certain he wouldn't continue with that area of study.

They pulled up to the house, a modern looking, sleek house, small but comfortable. The structure overlooked the Potomac River and the surrounding greenery. The two walked in and Ann showed Ahad to the kitchen, where Chris sat.

"Hey, Ahad!" Chris greeted. "How was the trip?"

Ahad shrugged. "Exhausting."

They all sat down at the kitchen table to discuss Ahad's next move. Their two dogs bounced around as Ahad walked in, but once they all settled into the kitchen, the dogs amused themselves elsewhere.

"So," Ann began as the two men got comfortable in their seats. "We need to map out what you need to do to stay here." When neither of the men responded, Ann continued. "You need to file for political asylum. The visa you have is expiring very soon so we need to file the application so we can get a temporary residency while they process your application."

Upon Ahad's blank expression, Chris clarified. "It basically means you'll be seeking refuge in the United States."

Ahad nodded. "So, how long will that take?"

"Depends," Ann wavered.

"We'll write any supplemental documents you need to pass through since we're citizens," Chris said.

Ahad nodded again. "And what will I be able to do when I file for political asylum?"

"You'll be able to get a green card, a work permit, find a job, attend a school." Ann shrugged. "Basically whatever you need to be a resident."

After a pause, Chris said, "It will definitely take some time. These things have to process and we have to organize everything. But it can be done."

"We'll be helping you with everything. We're familiar with these kinds of politics." Ann gave a reassuring nod.

The next hour or so was spent discussing their plan of action, possible timelines, and people they needed to see. It was a lot for Ahad to swallow but he did the best he could. He was going to need to get a hold of all this if he ever wanted to stay in the United States. He couldn't even begin to think about university until he found stable footing.

Ahad settled into the house quite well, though, within a

matter of days, he became restless. With Ann and Chris going off to work every day, Ahad coped with his boredom through menial tasks: making meals for the three of them, cleaning the house, walking the dogs. They took Ahad all around D.C. He tried so many kinds of food: Japanese, Indian, Mexican, the list went on and on. Ahad particularly liked the spices of Indian food since it reminded him of the bright flavors back home. The days dwindled past. Weekends were spent filling out forms to send to the Office of Immigration. Every time Ahad stepped outside, he was filled with a pressing, tense fear.

Each face he saw could have been someone after him. Each car that passed could have been a government official ready to grab him and deport him back to Afghanistan. Political asylum soon became the only thing left on his mind. Once granted political asylum, Ahad would be able to work, get schooling, find his own place in the United States. Ahad went to different doctors and dentists to strengthen his case for staying in the U.S. Ann covered all of the expenses and Ahad promised himself he would do whatever he could to help out. Ann also bought Ahad new suits and professional clothes for any possible interviews.

Ann and Chris wrote detailed letters pages long about Ahad's circumstances in Kabul. They described his connection to the American Cultural Center, his run in with the military, and how his entire life was threatened. If Ahad went back to Kabul, he would be killed. It was difficult for Ahad to fill out these forms. If Ahad was granted political asylum, he would never be able to go back to Kabul, back home. He would cut himself off from everything he'd grown up with. On the other hand, if he wasn't granted asylum…Ahad couldn't even begin to face that fact.

XXXIII
July 10, 1980
Washington D.C.

Ahad sat in the office, bouncing his leg up and down. In his hands, he held his transcripts as he looked at the man in front of him. Because Ahad's important documents were left behind in Kabul to avoid provoking questions, Ann was able to ship them to the United States along with her other possessions. When he applied for political asylum in March, the Office of Immigration gave him temporary residency permits since his visa expired in April. These permits allowed him to find a job and be schooled while waiting to hear the status of his application.

So much had changed in only a few months, though Ahad was grateful for the busyness. Ann and Chris took him out to parties, to meet friends, to better his English and he was slowly assimilating. Now, English didn't feel as foreign on his tongue. He became more accustomed to the food, even the seafood restaurants. He met different people and learned his way around D.C. Ann and Chris were also able to move back into their own house again. Now, the three were situated in a tall, four-story town home on 21st Street. Ahad took the bottom level apartment for himself and came and went frequently.

But no matter how much he occupied himself with housework or social events, political asylum was always on his mind. Sometimes, he would dream about getting deported back to Kabul, and as soon as he crossed the border, a line of soldiers would be standing there, rifles at the ready. Behind them, his entire family would stand in line, watching him. He saw his grandmother, who had died years before. He saw Omar looking at him with drooping, tired eyes. Ahad would take a step forward and then the guns exploded with a noise that startled Ahad awake. And there Ahad sat, in the bed of the townhome in D.C., still alive, still waiting.

He distracted himself from these fears with in-depth research about the colleges near him and found five schools to which he wanted to apply. Now, he sat in the Dean's office of Howard University.

The Dean's name was William Monroe, a tall man, respectable in appearance with a sharply coordinated suit and small beady eyes that scanned Ahad's face. Ahad recalled his previous visits to the other schools and he choked back a wave of panic. He had already met with the deans of these schools, hoping that he could start his master's program as soon as possible, but these visits were in vain. Meeting after meeting, Ahad's transcripts were rejected. Not because of his grades but because there was no way for any of the deans to validate the information. Kabul was as distant as Pluto to these people. Today was Ahad's last chance to be accepted into a university.

"Can you explain your circumstances to me again?" Monroe said.

Ahad debriefed his residency in D.C., his filing for political asylum, and the temporary residency documents that he received. Ahad handed over his schooling permit to Monroe, who inspected it for a solid two minutes. Each second put Ahad more on edge. He had to get in to this program. There was no other way for Ahad to land a dignified, well-paying job otherwise. No one would ever take him seriously. A degree from Kabul was about as useful as a handwritten recommendation letter from his mother.

"And you moved here from?" Monroe paused and glanced up from the documents to look Ahad in the face, "Kabul?"

Ahad felt very uncomfortable in his chair. The office seemed to be closing in on him. The air became thicker and the lights felt as if he were being interrogated.

"Yes, sir," Ahad said.

Monroe pressed his lips together then went back to examining the permit. Ahad wondered to himself what Monroe expected to find. Surely there wasn't enough information on that tiny piece of paper to keep Monroe occupied for that long.

"And what would you like to earn a degree for?" Monroe gave the paper back to Ahad.

"Computer science."

Monroe grunted and glanced down at the papers spread across his desk to what was plausibly student records or class availability. There was no telling what was on those papers so Ahad's mind immediately went to the worst possible scenario. Ahad's relationship with the Afghanistan military. Ahad's alleged reputation as a spy. Accounts from witnesses who saw Ahad cross the border illegally. The endlessness of those possibilities took root in Ahad's mind and would not budge. Maybe the Office of Immigration forwarded Ann and Chris's letters that detailed Ahad's history. That wouldn't exactly give him the appropriate reputation as a prospective student.

"Can I see your transcripts?" Monroe held out his hand, still not lifting his gaze.

As he placed the faded papers in Monroe's hand, Ahad held his breath. Several minutes passed while Monroe looked between Ahad's transcripts and the mysterious papers on the desk. Ahad could hear his own heartbeat, the sounds from outside of the office were vividly loud. The air felt thin, as if Ahad was winded. The last time he felt like this was when he first climbed to the top of the truck back at the Pakistan border.

Monroe lifted his head and met Ahad's gaze. Ahad searched for any sign of what Monroe would say, but Ahad still couldn't prepare himself for what came next.

"We can't accept these transcripts."

Ahad's breath caught. His chest tightened, his mind dulled to a shallow hum. Every muscle in his body tensed. Blood drained from his face, Ahad could do nothing but stare at Monroe, who seemed to resemble a snake: his pointed face, the beady slanted eyes, the unpredictable demeanor. Ahad fell back on the only reasoning he had left.

"Sir, these are completely valid. I can translate them if you need me to." Ahad found it difficult to speak. He tried to level his voice, but there was no use. Every part of Ahad was shaking.

"There's no need, we can't accept them." Monroe held out the papers to Ahad, who remained still.

"What if you let me attend for one semester and if I get As I can stay at the school? Surely that would be enough to prove my transcripts are credible." At this point, Ahad sounded like he was begging. There was nowhere else. The rejection he faced from the other schools was bad enough but this was Ahad's last chance. This was the only way Ahad could thrive in the United States.

Monroe said nothing and continued to hold out the papers. After a pause, Ahad lifted his hand to take his transcripts back. His arm felt heavy, his joints stiff.

"I'm sorry, but that's not possible. We have very limited seats and we can't negotiate to take a risk." Monroe's words rung in Ahad's ears. Every part of Ahad felt a bone crushing disappointment.

Ahad could find no other words except, "I understand." And he walked out of the Dean's office and off the campus to where Ann and Chris waited to pick him up.

XXXIV
December 4, 1980
Washington D.C.

Facing the facts was tough. Ahad felt as though he was back to where he started. Horrified of the future. This was exactly what he felt back in Kabul. He had thought he could finally shed that fear once he arrived in the United States. But there he was, standing outside Ann and Chris's new home, afraid of what would come next. With no degree in the United States, Ahad's chances of finding a well-paying job were slim.

Ahad had no other choice but to drown himself in research. He looked at every possible option of what could be his next move. Even though he had a work permit, it would be difficult to find a good job with little to no experience. Instead, he looked at short programs to give him some reliability as an employee. So he found the Computer Learning Center, the CLC, a short six month program in Springfield, Virginia. There, Ahad would be able to become a Computer Programmer or a Computer Operator, and then land a job in the computer industry. It was the best he could do.

Ahad applied for the program and for financial aid and could have sworn his heart almost stopped when he submitted his application. He prayed he would get enough money to pay for the program because Ann and Chris had already done enough for him. He didn't have the heart to take even more. He could find a job after attending the program and pay off the loan with his own money. It was nothing compared to everything Ann and Chris gave Ahad, but it was the best Ahad could do.

Ann and Chris had been immensely supportive. They helped Ahad through everything he needed and were always there to make Ahad feel at home. They took Ahad out and introduced them to more of their friends, showed him around the city, took him to their favorite restaurants. Although eternally grateful for all of their help, Ahad didn't want to be dependent on them anymore. Not only did it make him feel as though he was useless, but it made him feel guilty for taking so much from two of his closest friends and not being able to do anything in return.

There was always uncertainty in Ahad's life, especially in the last few years, but Ahad let his guard down. He thought he had found strong footing in D.C. and had hoped and expected to study in the United States. But rejection slapped him in the face. So Ahad turned to God, and gave up all control to Him. Ahad couldn't let himself be disappointed like that. Being rejected allowed Ahad to realize he needed to get a realistic grip on what was happening. It wasn't getting easier, a fact Ahad now understood, and all he could do was pray and do what was right in the name of Allah.

Ahad was at the mailbox again, a task he took upon himself to feel busy when he saw a letter from the CLC in Springfield, Virginia. He rushed inside and opened it. Ann and Chris were both at work. When he ripped open the envelope, his breath caught. Every part of his body started to shake. A surge of excitement rushed over him when his eyes saw the word "Congratulations."

He could barely contain himself. He felt like sprinting across the city, screaming at the top of his lungs. With no one to tell, Ahad left the house to walk around D.C., a huge grin spread across his face.

XXXV
1971
Kabul, Afghanistan

Ahad wore the mittens and hat his mother had sewn for him. He was about to leave for the annual week-long hunting trip he would always take with his father to Mazar-e-Sharif in the northern part of Afghanistan that drew ducks, geese, and swans to it during winter. Qadir was a serious hunter. He had a sleek expensive rifle that could shoot from kilometers away. Ahad's aim wasn't a great as Qadir's, but he was getting there. Now that he was in high school, Ahad was able to really focus on his body, his shot, and the feeling of satisfaction after collecting his game.

They traveled through the Hindukush Mountains in the tunnels that connected the north to the south. The weather was harsh, freezing, and there was enough snow year round for the Westerners to ski down the mountain slopes.

Ahad and Qadir got up long before the sunrise to go hunting and stayed with some close family friends who lived in the towns nearby. Around 3AM every day that week, Qadir shook Ahad awake to get ready to leave. They had hot milk and bread for breakfast to hold them over for the day. After packing up a few pieces of bread and dried melon, they rode horses over to a nearby lake. The horse Ahad rode was tall and dark, almost blending in with the night. The frigid air dried out his lips and made his eyes water, but there was no other feeling like it as he rode down the fields and over the hills with his father.

Ahad remembered when he struggled to ride a horse. Qadir had to lift him up, teach him how to direct the horse: right, left, stop. However, after growing a few centimeters, riding a horse was like second nature.

They trotted along the path until the lake slid into view. The water reflected the bright moonlight, and gently rippled onto the bank. Qadir glanced around. He had the same hooded eyes as Ahad and held a demanding presence. Any kid who came across Qadir wouldn't dare disrespect him. He led Ahad over to a tree a little ways off from the lake and dismounted, Ahad following in suit, and tied their horses to the trunk. They walked the rest of the way to the lake since the horses would scare off all of the birds.

Ahad could tell the sun was just about to rise so they took their positions near the edge of the lake, half obscured by grasses, and lay down onto the ground, their guns extending from their figures like extra limbs. The sun came up. A few geese waddled over to the water.

"Ready?" Qadir whispered, adjusting the barrel of his rifle to point at the birds ruffling their feathers. It was more of a command than a question, and Ahad made sure his gun was loaded and his hands were steady. Qadir always let Ahad take the first shot, a small gesture, but a kind one nonetheless. Ahad had improved greatly over the past few years and he was able to control the adrenaline he felt when pulling the trigger. There couldn't be any feeling inside him that could possibly screw up the shot.

Ahad adjusted his rifle, expelling the nerves in his chest. *One.* A deep breath. *Two.* The goose in line with the barrel. *Three.* The trigger. A loud noise shattered the peaceful dawn and a jolt ran through Ahad's body from the momentum of the gun. Ahad's eyes reflexively closed and when he opened, the goose laid near the bank, limp like a childhood doll of his sister's, blood dripping from the wound in its chest.

Ahad let out a small puff of air, relief, a smile. He looked over at his father, who wasn't looking at Ahad, but a grin wide across his face. The rest of the day brought around similar results. It was a particularly good day, and they brought back about a dozen birds. The family they stayed with cleaned up a few birds, two or three, and cooked them with steaming *basmati* rice and potato *korma* with freshly baked bread. Those were some of the best meals Ahad had ever eaten. The meat rich and tender, the bread flaky, steam rising from the rice and *korma*, infusing the house with blended smells of curry and onion, a smell Ahad would never forget.

XXXVI
January 5, 1981
Springfield, Virginia

Ahad finally got his driver's license. It took a few tries to pass the test, but he was glad to get it out of the way. Now, he could drive himself to the CLC since it was a little over half an hour from D.C. After he had gotten his license, Ann and Chris gave Ahad their Toyota car, a gold color with barely any scratches. To others, the car would appear unimpressive, but to Ahad, this car was the greatest thing he had ever seen. The fact that Ann and Chris gave him something as valuable as a car for no money at all bewildered Ahad. He was reluctant to take it at first. It seemed to him that Ann and Chris were an endless outpour of generosity. But after some persuading, the couple finally got Ahad to keep the car.

Now, Ahad stood by his car. *His* car. It was pleasing to think that. It was Ahad's first day at the CLC, and a sort of nervousness stuck with him, like the feeling of static. He had only felt like this when he first went to college in Kabul or when he had his first real soccer game at his high school. However, nervousness like this was a relief to Ahad compared to the fear that had stuck to him over the past year. He felt excited. Like a little boy.

After saying a quick goodbye to Ann and Chris, Ahad was off. The drive there felt quick. The minutes passed by as Ahad focused on the road. His mind ended up wandering and a rush of memory flooded him. He remembered being in school, spending time with his friends, fooling around in classes, the carelessness of being young. Ahad was still young but after this entire experience, Ahad felt as if he'd aged twenty years. He came to the United States a new man and began to look at everything in a new way. When he was a student back in Kabul, Ahad was spontaneous and wild. He was more worried about having fun than doing his schoolwork. Now, school was the only thing Ahad could think about.

When he pulled into the CLC, the morning sun was bright in the cloudless sky. He stepped out of the car, and was greeted with a gust of brisk wind. His breath clouded in the air and before going in, Ahad pulled out a cigarette and had a smoke.

Ahad sat in a classroom with adults of varying ages. The nervousness he felt before had now returned. The teacher was young, even younger than Ahad. However, Ahad listened attentively as he began to go over the lesson plans for the next six months. First, everyone would take an aptitude test to see if they would be learning to become a programmer or an operator. Taking in the information, Ahad saw himself at that moment. In a classroom. In the United States. He would graduate from this program. He would get a job. He would find his place. Nothing had ever sounded as sweet.

XXXVII
June 19, 1981
Washington D.C.

The feeling of graduating was renewed and fresh. It wasn't a traditional graduation or a traditional school, but Ahad was still overwhelmed with excitement and pride. He rooted himself in the United States. It was only onward from there. Ann and Chris came to support Ahad, and Michael called in to give his congratulations. Ahad and Michael had talked often since parting, updating each other about their lives.

The past six months were busy, to say the least. Ahad drove to the CLC every week day from D.C. and it soon became clockwork. The lessons at the school came to Ahad easily as well. From the University of Kabul, Ahad knew some background of how computers worked. But he drank in the new information each day. Eventually, he found a job on the campus. He was making a little money and getting more experience in the computer operating field. For the first time in months, Ahad felt hopeful.

Ahad was now at home in D.C. Later that night Ann and Chris planned to take Ahad out to a nice restaurant downtown to celebrate. Even though he had just finished the program, Ahad was eager to get his name out there. He wrote up a resume on a large cube computer tucked into the study of the house, typing up his name, his education, his work experience. He attached copies of his transcripts and immigration status. After asking for a fresh pair of eyes, Chris combed through it and refined a few phrases and words, then Ahad was set to go.

It was difficult to find available job positions. At this time in the year college students had already graduated and taken jobs around the city. There were no spots available in any computer companies in D.C. so Ahad reluctantly expanded his search to include Virginia. He would rather stay somewhere in D.C. since he would have to commute until he had enough money to live on his own. But after more searching, Ahad found an opening in one or two businesses to be a computer operator. Ahad immediately sent his resume and application. He found a few other companies with similar positions and soon all the names started to blend together. In a small notebook he scribbled down the places he had sent his application. Now it was the waiting game.

About a month had passed. Ahad was going in and out of interviews and sending out more and more applications once rejections started piling up. The companies to which he applied either outright denied him or Ahad applied too late and the position was filled. Finally, when Ahad received a call from Burroughs's Computer Corporation in Tyson's Corner, a whole new path opened up for him. He was elated, ecstatic; Ahad didn't even have enough words to express how excited he was.

He accepted the position graciously, spitting out a million thank yous to the manager who had called him. He would start the upcoming Monday for an annual starting salary of seventeen thousand. After hanging up the phone, Ahad was out of breath and sat down in the nearest chair to wrap his head around what had just happened. He could barely remember the phone call he'd just had. But he did it. He found a job, a *paying* job! Soon, Ahad would be able to move from Ann and Chris's house and depend on himself. That wouldn't be for a while, though. He would first need to save money and repay his friends who had given him so much. It was a lot to process.

But Ahad was here. After two years of living in constant

fear, Ahad found stable footing. He was here, but his family was not. Now that Ahad was in a secure position, he could help bring his family to the United States. He had been in distant contact with them since arriving but it was tricky to navigate the mail since all letters were searched thoroughly in Kabul. So, Ahad bought birthday cards and peeled off the extra layer of paper inside to write about his arrival in the U.S. The message was hidden well enough to pass unnoticed. Soon, he would help his family plan their own trip. Ahad was finally in a position to help.

With his job, Ahad could let go of the guilt induced by Ann and Chris's generosity. Soon, he could move out and feel more capable in the United States. Being sheltered for so long was driving Ahad insane.

Although endlessly grateful for all Ann and Chris had done, Ahad missed knowing his own way around town. In Kabul, he knew the street vendors; he knew his classmates; he knew the best areas to play soccer or ride his bike; he knew the food, the smells, the sights. In the United States, he felt like a little boy again, constantly protected and controlled. He was ready to initiate things on his own. He was ready to be independent again.

And that independence…what would Ahad even do with that kind of power in the United States? His mind was still too scattered to even begin thinking about his personal life. But as he sat there, in the small apartment on the bottom floor of Ann and Chris's house, the idea of settling came to his mind. Maybe he would be able to get married, start a family. Though the idea of having children terrified him. How would he ever raise them? He barely knew his own way around the United States. His children wouldn't be Afghan; they would be American.

The thought quickly vanished as he heard the door to the house unlock. At that moment, he was only focused on Ann's reaction to his first job.

XXXVIII
May 27, 1983
Washington, D.C.

"Hey, Ahad," Ann said. The three were in the kitchen, preparing dinner and Ahad stood at the counter chopping onions. Chris gladly passed that task over since Ahad's eyes didn't even water when chopping them.

"Yeah?" Ahad replied.

"So some of our friends from Idaho are going to come over next week for a conference. They're also bringing an exchange student. We thought it would be nice to have them for dinner. She's from Sweden, I think?"

She glanced over to Chris who added, "Finland."

"Finland," Ann repeated.

"That sounds great." Ahad nodded. "How long will they be staying?"

"I'm not sure. I'll have to ask. But it'll be a great time. They're very sweet people. Though we aren't going to be here since we're on a trip those days. Is that okay with you?"

"Absolutely."

The night continued on with light chatter. The past year Ahad was in and out of the house, going to his job at Burroughs's. After about six months at that company, Ahad moved onto the APA in Arlington, Virginia, where he was working currently. He set up a bank account for his paychecks and was earning a small sum of money to help buy meals, groceries, and other supplies for the house. The rest of the money was paying off his school loan. In a month or two he would move out and find a roommate. It was exciting but also bittersweet. He would most likely be moving to somewhere in

Virginia to be closer to his job which meant he wouldn't be as in touch with the two, but after everything they had been through, Ahad wasn't worried about losing contact. They were all too close for that now.

The week had passed by uneventfully. Ann and Chris were gone on their trip and that night, the family and exchange student were coming over to have dinner with Ahad. There were two spare rooms on the second floor of Ann and Chris's home that were cleaned thoroughly until they looked like an image on an advertisement.

Ahad decided to cook that night and was prepping his ingredients for a roast when he heard the doorbell ring. Ahad was got to the door and when he opened it, he was met with the face of a beautiful blonde girl. Her face was thin and her nose pointed. Her hair was a soft blonde that rested elegantly on her shoulders. After seeing her eyes, something stirred in his chest. They were a bright green, and although she was young, there were years of experience staring back at Ahad. The feeling he got was unexplainable. He was so lost in his thoughts that everything around him started to melt away.

She stood there, as still as Ahad. They stared at each other, unblinking, unfazed. Ahad's stream of thought was interrupted by the voice of a man behind her.

"So, can we come in?"

Ahad shook his head and laughed. "Yes, of course, sorry." Stepping aside to let everyone in, Ahad's eyes followed the girl. She must have been the exchange student. Something about her threw Ahad off track. It was a feeling he couldn't shake off. No matter how hard he tried, his mind kept steering toward her.

"Hi, you must be Ahad," the woman said.

Ahad nodded. "Yes I am. And you must be Delilah."

She nodded. "Ahad, this is my husband, John and our exchange student Sari."

Ahad shook John's hands politely. "Nice to meet you." Then Ahad looked at Sari and extended his hand. She was shy, and tucked her chin down, letting her hair cover her face as she shook Ahad's hand. Ahad grinned as he caught a glimpse of her smile. And in that moment, Ahad felt the fears of settling dissolve. For some reason, he knew that this girl would change his life. After everything, leaving his home, crossing the border, risking his life, looking at Sari made him feel at home again. And not those feelings of nostalgia when he saw Saleem or caught waves of memories from Kabul. He had that feeling there, in that moment, in the United States. And the night continued on, Ahad's chest buzzing with warmth.

EPILOGUE
January 25, 2018
Towson, Maryland

All my life, I saw my dad as this untouchable figure of strength and determination. I've always admired him for the stability he brought to the family. And over the past year, I realized there is no one else I could rely on to be as dependable as my father. I always know he will be there. It has been a constant aspect of my life that, admittedly, I've taken for granted.

Writing this book was more than just telling his story. In fact, there were things about my dad I never even knew until I took the time to sit down and listen to his stories. He became a whole new person to me. Looking at him now, I can only feel an immense amount of love and respect. I never understood how much he had sacrificed to get here. And I don't mean just getting to the United States. I mean *here*: with his family, a wife, and two daughters. A good and respectable job. The enormity of what he left behind astounds me and makes me feel nostalgia for a place and people I have never experienced.

I understand now that I will never be able to grow up the way my dad did. I will never get to experience the memories he held onto from Afghanistan. The Afghan dishes we eat now are only a faint echo of the enriched culture in which my dad grew up. I can't even begin to fully understand his life.

Being the first American generation is something that has ultimately influenced every decision I have ever made. It has broadened my global perspective in a way too abstract to even describe. However, it's something I've learned to be grateful for, because as the new generations come into the world, they are one step further from the understanding of my dad's life and the lives of people who have experienced the same.

These stories are only reminiscent of what he experienced. And I write them not just to document his amazing journey but to keep the essence of those experiences alive. The place we all have within history is incomprehensible. My dad was just one of the countless people who have gone through similar experiences. These people leave everything they have ever known to live a better life.

I always thought my dad left to come to the United States, but in writing this I realized it was so much more important than that. He didn't just leave to save his own skin. He left to protect his family and to be able to have the chance to build another family. I still haven't processed exactly how much responsibility I'm carrying. The expectation will always be there and in no way is it negative. In many ways, this expectation is self-imposed.

I expect myself to live out a life worthy enough of the sacrifices my dad made. I wasn't born to ignore the fact that my dad gave up absolutely everything to build a stable future for me and my sister. I will always have this standard that I'm reaching to meet. Everything I do will be to help fulfill the expectations of being the first American generation.

But I know there are many ways that I've already met this standard. Being aware of what my dad went through is compensation enough. I will always carry his stories with me, I will always carry some of the pain he experienced when leaving, and I will always have a piece of myself in Kabul even though I have never been there and probably never will be.

Even if I did have a chance see the city, it would be so far from the Kabul in which my dad grew up. I can only imagine what it's like now. The streets wrecked, the people living in constant fear. There is so much political tension that Afghanistan is barely habitable anymore. The idea of home there has probably diminished. And that is absolutely heartbreaking.

From here I can only move forward and listen when my pen calls me to write. I don't think I will ever be done telling my dad's story. And my mom's story is a whole other book in itself. I'm on my way to comprehending the deep history of my family, but the journey is only beginning. The path will be long and confusing and I will always turn to writing to help me make sense of it all.

As for now, all I can advise is to value the life you have, the family and friends around you. The things we take for granted are always the most valuable aspects of our lives. Do whatever you can to live the most meaningful life you can, because you never know who sacrificed everything they had to get you where you are today.

ACKNOWLEDGEMENTS

I would like to start out by thanking my family for supporting my wild endeavors and dreams. I wouldn't be who I am without you all.

Thank you to my father, Ahad, for the stories on these pages and everything in between. Thank you for reading through my words and making sure I get all the details right. This story is what it is because of you.

Thank you to my mother, Sari, for bringing me the encouragement and the excitement I needed when times got tough.

Thank you to my sister, Yasmine, for the advice and sanity. You kept me level-headed when I was too lost in the words.

Thank you to my friends, those who have helped me in and out of the classroom, especially the Literary Arts class of 2018. There's nothing better than walking into the classroom and seeing your wonderful faces.

Thank you to Lauren Goodwin, for always being there and for giving me generous amounts of positivity and support.

Thank you to Caroline Hein, for designing my cover, being so patient, and making my visions a reality. Thank you to Mr. Afshari and Mr. Newton, as well, for the insights and advice.

Thank you Mrs. Mlinek for helping me find my voice and giving me stable footing to walk this journey.

Thank you Mrs. Supplee for editing the endless amount of pages, for the passion you had for the story, and for the support and love you have given me.

And finally, thank you to everyone reading and keeping these stories alive.

ABOUT THE AUTHOR

Angie Faieq was born in Columbia, Maryland, and grew up with her mother, father, and sister. She spent her childhood reading any book she could get her hands on and writing her own whimsical stories. She attended her high school, G.W. Carver Center for Arts and Technology, for the Literary Arts magnet program and has been recognized as the Maryland State Champion for the 2017 Poetry Out Loud Competition, an experience she considers one of the most valuable in her writing life. Though, she has only just begun her writing journey and has many plans for future books.

94505131R00086

Made in the USA
Columbia, SC
28 April 2018